FUNNY HOW
THINGS CHANGE

MELISSA WYATT

FUNNY HOW
THINGS CHANGE

Farrar, Straus and Giroux • New York

Copyright © 2009 by Melissa Wyatt
All rights reserved
Distributed in Canada by Douglas & McIntyre Ltd.
Printed in September 2010 in the United States of America
by RR Donnelley & Sons Company, Harrisonburg, Virginia
Designed by Irene Metaxatos
First edition, 2009
10 9 8 7 6 5 4 3 2

www.fsgteen.com

Library of Congress Cataloging-in-Publication Data
Wyatt, Melissa.
    Funny how things change / Melissa Wyatt.— 1st ed.
        p.   cm.
    Summary: Remy, a talented, seventeen-year-old auto mechanic, questions his decision
to join his girlfriend when she starts college in Pennsylvania after a visiting artist helps
him to realize what his family's home in a dying West Virginia mountain town means
to him.
    ISBN: 978-0-374-30233-7
    [1. Interpersonal relations—Fiction.   2. Mountains—Fiction.   3. Country life—West
Virginia—Fiction.   4. Artists—Fiction.   5. West Virginia—Fiction.]   I. Title.

PZ7.W9683 Fun 2009
[Fic]—dc22

2008016190

To Jack Wyatt
and his West Virginia

FUNNY HOW
THINGS CHANGE

ONE

On his arm—just above his left hand—were three black letters. He'd put them there himself when he was twelve, him and Jimmy, done with coal dust pounded in with a nail drove through a stick. They never thought it would be permanent. But there it was, nearly five years on, his initials, R.A.W.

Lately, that's how Remy Walker felt. Raw on the inside, raw on the outside. Lying beside Lisa in the deep shade of the woods, her long limbs tangled with his, he wondered if she could feel it too, feel it burning through her own skin. It had been coming on for some time, coming with the end of their last year of high school, changing everything. Remy wished things could just go on the way they always had done, but something seemed to be pulling at him, like a persistent nudge to wake when you wanted to stay asleep. But waking up meant facing reality, that Lisa was leaving, going away, and he would be left behind.

All around them, the late June air hung so sultry, Remy couldn't tell it from his own hot, damp skin. No breeze moved the leaves and the only sound was the drone of insects, and some-where not far enough away, the shuddering impact of blasting. Remy flinched, turning his head instinctively. The top of another mountain—another lush green haven like this one—was going down to fast and dirty mining methods.

Lisa inched along the blanket she'd spread on the ground and put her lips to his ear.

"Come with me," she whispered.

"Where to?" he asked, her warm breath raising gooseflesh down his left side.

"To Pennsylvania, when I go to college." She kissed his ear. "You could come along."

He laughed and reached to break off a twig of spicebush. She was daydreaming, that's all. It was an easy place for it, out here in the woods, this place nobody else knew but them, all wrapped in green and each other. He wasn't going to college, but she was. Something that had been a blurry speck in the distance and was now just months away. He waved the spicebush twig under her nose. But she brushed it away and pushed herself up, looming be-tween him and the canopy of trees that covered them, her pale hair so long it trailed across his chest.

"Seriously, come with me," she said.

They'd talked about it before, lots of times. Sometimes joking, what it'd be like, what kind of apartment they'd get, how they'd stay up all night if they wanted and there'd be nobody to tell them what to do. Even when it was serious, it'd seemed a million years away, and for Remy, it had always had the safety of that distance, only now here it was, their last summer, and Lisa wanted to make the daydreams real.

"Oh yeah. I'll major in front end alignments." He drew her hair across his face, smooth against his lips, sweeter than the spicebush.

"I don't mean go to college." She stiffened against him. "Though you *could*. You know you could."

She'd bought completely into the higher education salvation preached at school. Get up, get out. That was their answer to being poor in West Virginia. Don't stay in West Virginia. At least don't stay in the mountains.

"Honey, I don't want to."

"Okay, but you could get a job." She wrapped her arms tight around his chest, like he might fly away. "There are gas stations in Pennsylvania, same as here. We'll get an apartment near the college. Remy, think! It's everything we always talked about! We could do it. We really could."

She was right. It was what they'd fantasized about. Get up, get out. Leave. She was every reason to say yes, he'd known it since that day back in tenth grade when she'd sat next to him in history class, crossed her silky legs, and smiled. He'd been saying yes ever since, rewarded with the head-spinning awesomeness of knowing she'd chosen him. And if he loved her, he shouldn't even have to think. The chance to be with her was the only thing that mattered.

She brushed his hair off his forehead with her fingers and held his eyes with hers.

"Remy, I can't imagine not being with you," she said. "Leaving Daddy and Momma and even this place is one thing, but not you. Not when we can do something about it."

Another muffled blast and Remy thought he felt the earth shake under them.

"Come with me," she said again, and everything around them was still, silent, waiting.

"Okay."

Because he had to be with her. He knew that much.

"Really?" She pushed up again, staring at him.

"Yeah, really. Let's do it."

His decision washed over him, leaving him feeling slightly drunk or like he'd just stepped off a cliff. And the joy that spread across her face reached out and caught him, held him up. He felt a laugh rise in his throat, a kid's laugh, and he didn't feel raw at all anymore. He felt like he could crack the whole mountain himself, if he wanted to.

"Remy, baby."

That was all it needed. He grabbed Lisa and pulled her down again, his face in her neck, her hair everywhere. Her lips met his and her fingers slid into his hair. He felt the soft warmth of her spread across him, like she could melt into him, pushing away that gasping feeling of having made such a big decision.

"It's getting late," Lisa breathed in his ear. "Aren't you working today?"

He swore, sat up, his head swimming with burning and kisses and plans. There were a lot of plans to be made, people they'd have to tell. Like his dad. His dad was going to hate this. But Remy pushed everything down with an almost physical effort and grabbed his shirt and skinned it over his shoulders.

"Remy?" Lisa's voice rose with uncertainty. "Are you okay?"

"Yeah." He hunted around for his boots. "Yeah, I'm okay. It's just . . ."

"Don't worry!" She smiled. "It's going to be great! Perfect."

She understood him, knew how he felt without him having to say. He held her, his hand behind her head, feeling the surprising strength of the slim tendons of her neck against his fingers. His heart still picked up speed when he looked at her. That day in tenth grade might have been the moment she decided he was worth noticing, but it wasn't the first time he'd noticed her. Long before that, every time he passed her in the halls at school or saw her on the streets in Dwyer, he felt like he was looking at a prize that was way out of his reach. So that day in history class, they both knew. It wasn't even a question.

He kissed her again. She soothed him in ways she didn't even know. She'd like that. He ought to tell her, but he didn't want to risk breaking whatever spell she cast without knowing it. His lips still touching hers, he fumbled with his shirt, buttoning it blind.

"I gotta go," he told her. "I'm covering Jimmy's—" Kiss. "—shift tonight and then I'm—" Kiss. "—on again in the morning. I'll see you tomorrow afternoon, maybe."

"You staying in the bottom tonight?"

"Yeah," Remy grunted as he jerked on the laces of his scuffed boots. "If Duff'll let me sleep in the garage."

He didn't have a car and it was nearly an hour's hike from Duff's Gas and Go down in the creek bottom at the north end of town all the way up Walker Hollow to where he lived with his dad on the mountain south of town. Not worth the effort when he was pulling a double shift.

"Let me drive you to work," Lisa said, brushing off bits of leaves and pine needles from her tank top.

"No time." He grabbed her wrist and tapped the face of her watch. "You gotta go get Scott."

Scott was her little brother, waiting to be picked up from swimming lessons at the park pool, the opposite direction from where Remy was headed.

"Oh damn, that's right." She jumped up and they hiked down the mountain to her mother's car, where she bundled the blanket into the trunk. "Well, it won't be long and we'll be together all the time, just us, in our own place."

Looking at her, Remy thought how cute she was with her hair tousled and her makeup all kissed off. How lucky he was, how lucky he'd be to get to see her like this every day.

"You're beautiful," he said.

"Oh, go to work!" She put her hands flat on his chest, gave him a little shove, and climbed into the car.

"See you tomorrow." He kissed her again through the rolled-down window and stood back to watch her drive off before he started on his own way.

Sweat was rolling down Remy's back by the time he hauled himself over the guardrail onto Route 25. Ordinarily, he wouldn't have minded. He liked the walk along the highway, with the mountain rising on one side and the valley and the town spread out on the other, liked the sense of walking halfway between the two. But now his mind buzzed with thoughts he couldn't smack down. Mostly about telling his dad he'd just decided to up and leave. It would cut them both, his dad more than him because his dad would be alone. But it was no good thinking about that. Better to think about Lisa, the smell of her still clinging to his skin, like she was part of him even when she wasn't there.

The highway had been cut through the mountain more than fifty years ago and the rock was still bleeding water. Mostly, it only oozed steadily, covering the rock in a shiny glaze in summer and freezing into geologic formations in winter. But in some places, it made little waterfalls. If the outfall was low enough, people put in pipes and bottled the water for drinking. To Remy, it only proved that the mountains were alive—great living things with cool, clear water in their veins.

He stopped where a decent spring fell from an outcropping maybe fifteen feet over the road and stuck his head under the cascade of water. Even in mid-June, the water was cold enough to make him shout at the shock of it on his neck. He threw back his head and let it splash over his face, steaming from the climb, felt it run down his chest and back, soaking his shirt.

"That looks great!"

Remy straightened, the water flattening his hair down over his forehead and running into his eyes, so that he had to step out of the fall, pushing dark hair and water out of his face, to see who had spoken.

It was a girl. On the other side of the road, she sat on a small scaffolding built around the front of the Dwyer municipal water tower, surrounded by cans of paint. How had he not noticed her? Or at least her car, a red Mustang convertible parked in the pullover that overlooked the town. He didn't recognize either the girl or the car. He felt stupid, like he'd been caught dancing in his underwear.

"Is it safe?" the girl asked. "Can you drink it?"

He looked at the steady stream of water, as if he could analyze it by squinting, and shrugged.

"I guess," he said.

"Oh, good."

She hopped down from the scaffolding and crossed the road. "I ran out of tea an hour ago and didn't want to go into town for something to drink. It takes so long to get anywhere down here!"

He could tell by the way she talked that she wasn't from any-place nearby. And that "down here" crack confirmed it. An out-sider. She held cupped hands under the water and bent over to drink. Remy could see that she wasn't as old as he first thought. A little older than him but not by much, maybe nineteen. Small and compact, like her car.

She smiled at him, water dripping off her chin.

"That's so good! Better than Evian. You ought to bottle this stuff and sell it."

She yanked off the bandanna that was holding back her short brown hair, held it under the water, and then wiped her face and neck, damp little curls clinging to her temples and the nape of her neck. When she raised her arms to tie the wet bandanna back over her hair, Remy caught himself staring.

What was wrong with him? He'd been with Lisa forever, it seemed. They'd known each other since they were kids, had both been virgins that night two years ago when they'd gone to the dugout behind the high school while most of the county was in-side watching the annual reenactment of the Rope River Mine War. He hadn't felt drawn to look at another girl like this. Why should he when he had everything he wanted?

The girl stared back at him, and he felt brown eyes flecked with green move over his face and follow the droplets of water that trickled down his body, running over the flat muscles between the two halves of his open shirt. He was made by the mountains, tall, thin, and wiry, his body shaped by years of climbing trees and rocks and the kind of physical work most people didn't think anyone had to do anymore, not in this country, anyway.

For a second, he had this crazy mental picture of kissing her, just taking hold of her and kissing her. Then a car swept by, close on their side, the draft kicking up hot air and dust, scaring the girl so that she took a bad step and slid into the rainwater gully.

Swearing, she scrabbled up, and Remy reached a hand to pull her back onto the road.

"You okay?"

"Yeah, thanks." She smacked dust off her bottom. "Serves me right for admiring the scenery when I should be working." She looked at him, squinting a little. "You live around here?"

"Close enough," he said.

She pointed at the black letters on his arm. "What's that stand for?"

He looked at his arm, like he forgot what was there. "Just my initials. Remington Alvin Walker, that's me."

"Remington?" Her eyes widened.

"It's a family name."

That's what his dad said, laughing and following it up with "Yep, that shotgun is like a brother to me." Part of his hillbilly put-on, like the stoneware jug he kept in the kitchen of their small trailer, telling visiting distant cousins it was full of moonshine when Remy knew it was only filled with Jack Daniel's, bought special for the occasion from the liquor store. Still, it wasn't always easy carrying around a joke as a first name. A lot of people took it seriously, thinking you were named after a gun. And outsiders—like the girl—either thought it was quaint or scary, neither of which felt especially good.

"Remington." She rolled his name over her tongue like she'd done with the water. "That is such a cool name. Very unique."

Nobody had ever thought it was cool. He gave the girl another look.

"I'm Dana Shaeffer," she said. "For no particular reason."

He nodded acknowledgment. "Where are you from?"

"I'm from Maryland, originally, near Washington, D.C. We moved to West Virginia, to the eastern panhandle, a couple of years ago because it was cheaper."

Yeah, he'd heard about that. It was supposed to be good for the state, to have these commuters move in. But all they did was drive up the prices so the local people couldn't afford to live there anymore.

"So what are you doing away down here?"

"I'm painting the water tower," she said.

He looked at her to see if she was kidding, but she seemed serious. "What for?" he asked. "Just been painted a year ago."

"Not that kind of painting," she said. "I'm painting a mural on it. Come and see."

He followed her across the road where she unfolded a big piece of paper with a picture drawn on it in pencil. It took a couple of minutes of hard staring to figure out it was a jumble of important points in McGuire County history. There was the old county courthouse bigger and more impressive than it had ever looked, a train heaped with coal, the writer Rosella Banks, U.S. Senator John T. McGonaugle, the obligatory coal miner, and some mountains in the background.

"Did you draw this?"

"Mm-hm." She nodded.

He had to keep looking at her, his ideas about her shifting so quickly in such a short time.

"It's good."

"Thanks," Dana said.

"What's it for?"

"What do you mean, 'What's it for?' " she asked. "It's art. It's supposed to make you think. I'm doing four of these down here this summer. I've already done two up in Blair County. I won a grant."

"From who?"

"The state government." She rolled the picture back up.

"The state is paying you?" Remy asked. "To paint pictures on water towers?"

"Uh-huh. Not much, though. I was hoping to have enough so I could live off-campus when I go back to college in the fall. I *hated* living in the dorm. Not that my parents wouldn't help me out, but you know. I thought it would be cool if I could say I paid for some of it myself. My dad thinks majoring in art is a total waste of time. It'd be nice if I could show him I can make some money from it."

His ideas about her shifted again. A transplanted running-at-the-mouth Maryland rich girl, painting scenes of civic pride on the water towers of dying towns and getting paid by the state to do it.

"Yeah, well, see ya," he said and started back across the highway.

"You don't have to go!" she shouted after him. "Why don't you stay and talk to me?"

"Got to work," he said without turning. "I wouldn't drink any more of that water."

"Why not? You said it was okay."

13

"I said I guessed, but you never know. I heard they were starting mountaintop removal over on Jarrett Mountain this week. Heard blasting today. No telling where they're dumping the overload."

"What's that mean?"

He stopped in the middle of the road and turned around. "They tear the top off the mountain so they can get to the coal easier. Then they dump the waste down in the valley and the acid from the slag gets into the creeks and groundwater. Why don't you put that on the water tower?"

Her face went all red for a second, like she wanted to yell at him. Then she put her hands on her hips and said, "You want to explain to me how this is all my fault?"

"Take too long. I've got a job to get to. Some of us work because we have to, not because it's a cool idea."

He could hear her banging paint cans around the whole way down the bend and laughed with satisfaction. Maybe he shouldn't have told her that lie about Jarrett Mountain. The blasting he'd heard was miles away. The water was fine to drink. But there was something about her that pricked at him—being paid by the state to paint pictures, going crazy over the spring water, calling him "scenery" like he was only there for her personal viewing pleasure. Let her drive into town and pay for a drink.

TWO

Jimmy, what the Sam Hill did you do to this car?" Duff growled from under the hood of a '91 LeSabre.

"I fixed it." Jimmy had pulled the rattly old office chair out to the front of the garage and sat leaning way back, with his feet propped up on a tepee sign advertising low-tar, low-price, high-satisfaction cigarettes, drinking a Coke. He was off for the night, but had stopped by in his date clothes before he went to pick up his girlfriend.

"The damnation oil filter won't come out, Jimmy. You got it jammed."

"I can't help you," Jimmy said. "Kayla'll kill me if I come over all covered in grease. Make Remy do it. He's got them big coal-miner hands."

"Sorry. Got a customer."

Remy sauntered over to the big Japanese SUV that had pulled up to the pumps. Looked like it got rubbed down every night with a diaper, never been off-road in its life. The driver, a man in his fifties, got out and told Remy to fill it up with premium.

"Say, maybe you boys can help us." The man laughed. "I think we're a little lost."

"Where you trying to go to?" Jimmy asked.

"We've got reservations at the Black Bottom Resort."

"Never heard of it," Jimmy said. "Remy?"

"Nope," Remy said. "What's it near?"

"I think the nearest town is called Irlee." The man scratched his head, as if he could scratch up the name.

"Irlee's over in the next county," Remy told him.

"Is that far?" A woman leaned out the passenger window of the car.

"Everything's far down here." Jimmy tipped his Coke at her.

"Two hours, maybe." Duff came out from behind the LeSabre, wiping his hands on a grimy cloth.

"Two *hours*?" the woman nearly screamed. "We've been driving since dawn already! These mountain roads are making me feel nauseous."

"What can we do?" the man said. "We've just got to keep going."

The woman snorted. "Hurry up, then." She closed her window and sat back, steaming.

The man smiled weakly and handed Remy his credit card. "Beautiful country, these Blue Ridge Mountains. Almost heaven, just like the song."

"Uh-huh," Remy said. "Except this is the Appalachian Plateau. The Blue Ridge Mountains are in Virginia mostly."

"Is that right?"

Remy ran the card through the processor in the office and brought the receipt back out for the man to sign, then wrote out directions to Irlee.

"Thanks for your help, boys." The man waved and got into his car.

Jimmy hooted as they drove off. "Another victim of the tourism board. Come to wild, wonderful West Virginia—and get lost."

"Shut up, Jimmy," Duff muttered. "What are you doing here anyway? Thought you had a date."

"I do." Jimmy finished his Coke and tossed the bottle into the garbage. "Kayla don't get off work until six o'clock, and if I stay around home Mom'll hit me up for money, then I won't be able to take Kayla anywhere."

"Where you going, anyway?" Remy leaned against the gas pump. "Dressed up like that?" The closest date places—movie theaters, nice restaurants, clubs—were three hours away in Beckley. Mostly, people hung out and watched TV. Everyone had a satellite dish.

"We're going to Beckley. I got reservations at Kimballs."

Remy whistled. Kimballs was crystal and cloth napkins and jack all to pay for.

Jimmy stood up and patted the pockets of his pants nervously. "I—uh—I'm gonna ask Kayla to marry me."

Duff banged his head on the hood of the LeSabre.

"Jesus H. Jones!"

"Are you serious?" Remy straightened. "I mean, congratulations, Jimmy."

"So what brought this on?" Duff asked.

Jimmy shrugged. "We been going out a couple of years now. I figured it was about time." He gave Duff a level look. "She isn't pregnant, if that's what you're getting at."

"Good." Duff crammed his hand towel into his coveralls. "I raised you boys to be smarter than to let something like that happen. I'd hate to see all my good work go to waste."

At twenty-six, Duff was only six years older than Jimmy, nine years older than Remy, but he liked pulling rank on them, saying he'd taught them everything they knew—everything that was important, that is. In some ways, it was true. It was Duff who gave Remy his first condom, not his dad.

"All right, we gotta have a toast." Duff went into the office and came out with more Cokes and passed them around. Holding his out in front of him, he said, "To Kayla, poor unsuspecting girl. May she come to her senses and say no, but if she doesn't—well—let's hope she can stand the smell, anyway."

"All right, all right," Jimmy said. "She could do a whole lot worse."

"In this county, she couldn't do a whole lot better, but that ain't saying much," Duff said.

"You watching the time, Jimmy?" Remy asked.

Jimmy looked at his watch, swore. "I gotta go. I'll see you tomorrow, let you know what she said. Thanks for covering for me, Rem."

Duff went back to his engine and Remy stood and watched Jimmy's car pull away. He'd known Jimmy since grade school, when he was in first grade and Jimmy was in third. On Remy's first day of school, Jimmy'd stepped in and stopped a fight between Remy and another boy who was making fun of his name.

"Don't know if I'd make fun of somebody whose daddy named him after a *gun*," he'd said, and the kid had run off.

After that, they'd been together in discovering everything the mountains could offer. Climbing rocks and trees, tubing down ice-cold, rain-swollen creeks, trashing more bikes than they could count while riding down crazy steep hillsides, hunting for trilobites up on the escarpments, and eating pawpaws until they got sick.

And now Jimmy was getting married, another mark of things moving along, changing. Remy was glad to be going, glad he wouldn't be around to see everything shift.

The phone ringing made him jump.

"You wanna get that?" Duff yelled from back under the hood of the LeSabre.

Remy ambled into the office and picked up the phone. "Duff's Gas and Go," he said.

"Remy, is that you?" a woman's voice said. "It's Mom."

"Oh hey! How are you?" There was no phone in the trailer he shared with his dad, so his mom had to call him at the garage.

"I'd be better if I'd hear from you once in a blue moon," his mother said. "There's a reason I keep sending you those phone cards, you know."

"I know," he said. "I'm sorry. I've been working and stuff."

"Oh, sugar, I've heard it all before." She laughed. "I know what you've been busy with. Some girl, right?"

He didn't answer, let her laugh at him some more.

"But listen, angel," she went on. "I've been thinking now that you're out of school, why don't you come on down here and stay with me for a while? Hmm? Your daddy's had you long enough.

Come and relax and have some fun before you join the rat race."

His mom lived in Virginia Beach, and to her it was paradise. He'd gone with her at first when she left his dad, back when he was twelve. But to Remy, the beachfront hotels and shabby boarding-houses never felt like home. Even away from the tourist traps, the mudflats and tidal marshes were alien landscapes and the flat voices of the people another language. The sparse, salt-stunted trees seemed as uncertain as him how to grow there. So, after less than a year, his dad came and took him home. Home to the moun-tains. Only he'd never been able to get his mom to understand that he didn't see things her way, that he didn't think Virginia Beach was exactly a step up from Dwyer.

"Don't tell me you aren't ready to see a little of the world out-side of McGuire County now that you're a free man," his mom was going on in his ear.

What would she think if she knew about his fresh-made plans to follow Lisa? But he couldn't tell her before he told his dad. It wouldn't be fair. And she might be mad, too. Mad that he was leav-ing, but not heading her way.

"It sounds great," he said, as sugary as possible. "I'll think about it, okay? I don't know when I'd be able to swing it."

He'd need every bit of his money for his new plans. Couldn't afford to spend any on even a short visit to Virginia Beach. A blast from a car horn out front saved him.

"You just let me know, darlin'," she said. "You're always wel-come. Don't you forget that."

"I won't. I gotta go, Mom. I'll call you soon."

"You will not."

"I will. I swear."

He hung up and went back out front, where the red Mustang and its owner sat at the pump island.

"Well, if it isn't the director of public water safety," the girl said.

Remy walked over to the car, grinning. This girl had a smart mouth on her.

"Sorry about that," he said. "It was only a joke."

"Yeah, whatever. Just fill it up." She squinted at him. "If the gas is safe."

Remy stood at the gas tank with his back to the girl, looked over his shoulder once or twice and caught her watching him in the rearview mirror. He put the gas cap on and came back to her side of the car.

"That'll be forty dollars."

She handed him a credit card.

"The water's fine," he said. "Honestly. Don't be scared."

"I'm not scared." She stared hard at him. "I knew you were lying. I'm just not sure why."

"No reason."

"You said it would take too long to explain."

"It was a joke, honest." He smiled at her. "Want me to get you a Coke?"

"No thanks." She sniffed, tossed her curls around. "Is there anywhere to eat around here that doesn't involve biscuits and gravy? Someplace I could get a salad?"

"Why yes, ma'am." Remy leaned on the door of her car and drawled. "We got us a newfangled McDonald's t'other side of town. I done heered they got plastic forks and ev'rythang, like real civilized folks."

He gave her his killer smile. She was cute, real cute, trying hard not to smile back.

"Ha ha," she said. "Where is it?"

"On Hager Road." He gave her directions.

"I'll never find it. This place is so confusing. Can you show me?"

"I'm kind of working, here."

"You get a break for dinner, don't you?" she asked. "Can't you take it now, or are you overrun with customers?"

No. He oughta just say no. You didn't go to McDonald's with a girl like this, not when you loved your girlfriend the way he loved Lisa. You smiled and wrote down the directions for her. But while his brain was saying that, his mouth was saying something else.

"Well, if you're going to die if you have to eat a biscuit, I guess I'll have to come along." Remy's hand reached for the door handle. "Don't want that on my conscience."

He shouted to Duff that he was taking his break and climbed into the Mustang. The girl pulled out of the gas station before Duff could say anything.

"I forget your name," Remy said. "Turn right here."

"That's flattering. I remember yours."

"Sure, everybody remembers my name."

The car was very cool, the engine loud enough to sound hot. God, it must be nice to have something like that handed to you.

"Dana," the girl said. "My name's Dana."

"Stay on this road," he said as they came to the split where the road either went through town or up along the ridge. It'd be faster to go around town, but it would mean going by Lisa's house, something he'd like to avoid. Stupid, since she was probably out with her friends. And it wasn't like he was doing anything wrong. It was nothing, riding in a car with a girl, with Dana. It didn't mean anything. Still, he told her how to get through town.

At McDonald's, Dana went through the drive-through, and Remy carefully kept his head turned away when they got to the pickup window. He knew most everyone who worked there, and if he was spotted in a car with a strange girl it'd be all over town by morning.

"Where can we go to eat?" Dana asked. "I hate eating in the car."

"I don't have time. I only get a half an hour for dinner and we blew a good bit of that driving over here."

"Oh, come on," she said. "You can be a little late."

He'd never been late, ever. But suddenly it seemed like a great idea. Cut loose, have some fun, like his mom had suggested. Okay, maybe it wasn't quite what she had in mind, but right then, it was exactly what he wanted to do.

So he took her to the high school, way up on the mountain, away from the town and the lights that were beginning to come on.

"You brought me to a school?" she said, climbing out of the car. "What should I read into that?"

Only that it was the most farthest away place where he knew they wouldn't run into anyone he knew, especially on a summer evening.

"Did you go here?" Dana asked.

"Yeah." Funny how it seemed like an age ago, not hard to think of it in the past tense.

"Doesn't it feel weird to come back after you graduate?" She reached into the car for her food. "Everything is so much smaller than you remember."

But it still looked the same to Remy, only empty and echoing. A ghost town.

"I only graduated three weeks ago," he said.

"Really?" Her eyebrows shot up, and it was her turn to readjust her ideas about him. She laughed.

"What?" he asked.

"Nothing." She shook her head.

They walked around to the picnic tables outside the cafeteria. Across the ball field were the dugouts and a quick, warm memory of Lisa, but Remy hitched his bottom on top of the table and turned his back, concentrating on unwrapping his dinner.

Dana sat on the bench by his feet, a little closer than was absolutely necessary, so that her shoulder almost touched his calf, and ate a salad out of a plastic box.

"So this painting on water towers thing," Remy said, inspecting the toppings on his burger. "Is this a permanent gig or something?"

"What do you mean?" She squinted at him.

"Like what you want to do."

"You mean my goal in life?" She practically choked on her salad. "Not specifically water towers, no," she said, eyes watering.

"Maybe you could branch out into electrical substations," Remy said and grinned at her.

"A girl can dream." She took another bite. "But really, yeah, I mean I want to paint. But I want to paint things that are important to me, you know? I don't want to work in advertising or something. I want to make art that makes people think."

"Well, your water tower will sure make people around here think," Remy said. He didn't say what they'd think, though.

"I'll bet," was all Dana said.

She looked out over the town and took a deep breath, letting it out slowly, contentedly.

"It's so different here," she said.

"Different how?" Remy felt prickles rise. "Because it's not exactly like where you came from?"

"You don't have to get defensive on me." She pushed a forkful of salad into her mouth. "I didn't mean different-bad. I meant it's nice."

Remy laughed. "You should've stuck with different."

"Why?" she asked. "Don't you think it's nice here?"

Around them, the settling cool of evening came out of the trees on a breath of balsam. Remy inhaled it along with his burger, heard the sigh of leaves and the last-minute calls of birds, and somewhere far away a train whistling down the track, like background noise.

"It's all right."

"Wow," Dana said. "High praise."

She tipped her head back. "You have to look straight up here to see the sky," she said. "It makes me claustrophobic."

"That's because you're not used to it." Remy concentrated on his burger. "If you were, you wouldn't think about not being able to see past the next mountain. All that's on the other side is another mountain."

"That's pretty cynical." Dana straightened. "But you know it's not really like that. It's almost a challenge. That's what I felt the first day I came down here. The mountains are so beautiful, but they're not going to cut you any breaks. Do you know what I mean?"

"Yeah, I know what you mean. It's like these tourists that stopped at the garage today. They want to come down and see the mountains, but they don't want to have to put any effort into it."

"Yes! Even driving down here isn't easy."

"Or getting into town for an iced tea?" Remy teased.

"Yes!" She laughed. "But it's worth it, right? I mean, isn't that why people stay here, even though there's no place to shop and stuff? There's something else, isn't there?"

"I guess." Remy crumpled his sandwich wrapper and picked up his drink.

She played with her salad. "Have you always lived here?"

"Um-hm," he mumbled around his straw. "Except a couple of months, I lived with my mom in Virginia Beach. Now that was different."

"You didn't like it there?"

"Nope." But no way was he going to go into why with this girl. "Never was big on sand."

"I've lived in four different places," she said. "Mostly, though, they seemed pretty much the same. That's why different looks good to me. Where we live now, it's getting to be like where we left. As if they picked up the same neighborhood and plopped it down seventy miles away. Same houses, same stores, same people. It doesn't make sense when the whole point was to get away from that."

"Different didn't look so good a bit ago, when you didn't know where to get a salad," he said.

"There are some things you can't live without." She pointed

her toe toward the town. "Speaking of which, does everyone down here have satellite TV?"

Down in the valley, the houses and hillsides were studded with satellite dishes.

"West Virginia wildflowers, we call them," Remy said. "That is a thing you most definitely can't live without."

He leaned back, his hands splayed out on the table, thinking idly that he ought to get back to work instead of sitting here, flirting. He felt something brush his arm and looked down, startled, to see Dana tracing the three black letters.

"Do you have any more of these?" she asked.

"What? Initials?"

"No!" she said. "Tattoos. Got any more? In interesting places?"

For a second, he watched—almost fascinated—as her finger went down-up-down-up on the W.

"Nope." He pulled his arm away, covering the tattoo with his other hand and rubbing gently. "First one hurt too much to ever think about trying it again. When I'm dumb, I'm usually only dumb once."

What would she think if she knew where the tattoo had come from, how him and Jimmy saw that movie about the sailors in Tahiti and got inspired? Whose idea was it? He couldn't remember now. But he remembered how mad his mom was, how she threatened to take him somewhere and have it removed. How Jimmy chickened out when he saw the blood running down Remy's arm.

"Why?" he asked her. "How many tattoos do you have?"

"Wouldn't you like to know."

She'd climbed up on the table next to him and they sat, looking at each other. In the falling light, the map of her face was thrown into relief, all bright curves and deep shadows. A face that moved with her thoughts and ideas. He could almost feel her energy crackling across the table. Again, the thought of kissing her came, but different this time, not wanting to grab her, like he had up on the highway, but just to sway close enough to brush against her.

But then she swayed toward him and he panicked, getting up so fast he nearly fell on his backside.

"Don't hurt yourself," she said, laughing at him.

"I've got to get back to work," he said. "Or I won't be able to pay for any more fancy fast-food dinners."

They got in her car and he took her back along the highway this time, past her water tower. Remy frowned into the gathering dark, wondering if wanting to kiss another girl counted as cheating or if stopping yourself could be considered noble.

They didn't say much until Dana pulled into Duff's and Remy climbed out of her car.

"Are you working tomorrow?" she asked him.

"In the morning."

"What are you doing after work?"

Remy shrugged, but his words were deliberate. "Probably hanging out with my girlfriend."

"Oh," Dana said and stared through her windshield for a second. "Well, a friend of mine has a private cabin up at Painter Falls Park. I've been staying with him. A painter at Painter Falls!" She giggled. "Anyway, we're having a cookout tomorrow. Why don't you come up after work? You can bring your girlfriend."

"Your friend has a private cabin?"

"It's his parents' cabin. He's kind of a local, spends his summers here."

Kind of a local. Remy knew the type, but he let it go.

"Maybe we'll come. I don't know what my girlfriend wants to do."

"I know what I'd want to do if I was her." He wondered if he'd heard her right, but she kept talking. "It's cabin four. There's a map at the park office. Anytime after six." And she was gone.

Remy wandered into the office, feeling like once when he'd got caught in the rapids farther down on the Rope River and barely managed to pull himself up on the bank. Mixed up and stupid, but sort of wanting to do it again.

"Sorry I'm late, Duff."

"Huh?" Duff looked up from the carburetor he was cleaning, cradled in his lap like a pet dog.

Remy sat on the battered old desk.

"That's something about Jimmy asking Kayla to marry him, isn't it?" he asked Duff.

"It's something, all right," Duff said.

"I thought you were happy for him."

"Nothing else to be, since his mind is made up. Just don't let it put any ideas in your head."

The service bell rang and Remy went out front, surprised to see Dana.

"Thought I just filled you up," he said.

"Ohhhhh." Dana grinned at him. "There are soooo many places I could go with that."

He had to laugh. She was definitely cute. Cute and funny. He wished he could think of something really smart to say, but maybe it was better not to. He knew it was a game, and if he whacked the ball back over the net then everything after that was fair play.

"What can I get you?" he asked instead.

"Nothing. I've got something for you."

She fished down between the seats, pulled out a piece of paper, and handed it to him.

"Come tomorrow," she said. "I really want you to." She drove off with a toot of her horn.

Under the fluorescent lights of the pump island, Remy spread out the paper she'd handed him. It was a McDonald's bag and on the blank inside, a drawing. Of him. His head, anyway, a quick sketch in ballpoint pen, but he recognized himself right away. It was weird to think of her drawing him, remembering what he looked like enough after the short time they spent together. He didn't know what to make of her. But he folded the drawing and tucked it into his pocket. He knew he wouldn't show it to anyone.

THREE

It was Saturday and Remy knew that whatever Lisa and him decided to do that night, he had to get home and change clothes. He got lucky and caught a ride with a school friend who didn't have anything better to do but drive him up the hollow. The hollow—and the mountain—were named after his family, a long time back. Back before anyone thought of coal.

The first Walker to live there was a trapper, and Remy knew where to find the stone foundation of his tiny cabin. Used to play war up there with his cousin Dylan before Dylan's parents moved them away.

Now Walker Mountain was played out, not worth anything, everyone said. Remy was a little boy when he first heard someone say that, and thought it was the dumbest thing he ever heard. What was a mountain supposed to be worth, anyway?

To Remy, it was more than his home. It was woven through every memory he had. He knew every path, every glade, the course of the streams, and the biggest trees. Knew where to find wintergreen and wild ginger, had caught tadpoles and turtles and had risked broken bones on dares and crazy stunts on steep outcroppings and snake-haunted bottoms. He knew that mist in March smelled different than mist in June, and that mist in October was the smell of sadness. But none of that added up to what other people called value.

When his friend dropped him off at the end of Walker Hollow Road, Remy suddenly understood what those people meant. It was only a mountain. The other stuff, what did it matter anyway? It was over and done. He was done with Walker Mountain. Head down, he hiked up the hollow.

He hadn't been home in two days, but when he walked into the trailer, his dad didn't ask where he'd been.

"You ain't been arrested yet, have you?" his dad said once when Remy asked why he never checked up on him.

"No."

"Then I trust you not to be dumb enough to get in trouble now."

That's the way his dad reasoned. "If it ain't broke, don't fix it" was one of his favorite sayings. He had an undemanding way of doing things, of living, that mostly suited Remy.

His mom used to fuss constantly, telling them to keep their feet off the furniture and put things away and not drink out of the milk carton. But it had been so futile, her fussing. That's why she left.

"I give up! I can't live the way you live anymore," Remy had heard her shouting at his dad. "I've got to get out of this hole!"

His dad hadn't argued, had even sadly helped her pack up the good car like he was helping her pack for a voluntary trip to Hell.

"I wish you could be happy here," was all he said. "But I know this ain't what you want."

And his dad had gone on, living his own way, and he and Remy'd gotten along okay.

On this Saturday afternoon near the end of June, his dad sat at the kitchen table wearing a T-shirt and boxers because of the heat, smoking a cigarette and reading the newspaper. His three-inch beard was turning gray from the outside in and the creases around his eyes were permanently stained black with coal dust. He didn't have a regular job anymore. He'd been laid off from the Bluebird Mine when Remy was a little boy. These days, he went backcountry and dug coal out by hand and sold it, pickup truckload by pickup truckload. Sometimes he did carpentry work when he could find it—or when anyone could pay for it. Said he'd let the mountain drop on him before he'd go work at McDonald's or, worse yet, take a government handout. Stubborn, Remy's mother called it, and maybe it was.

"You want eggs, Remy? I'll make you some."

"Yeah, okay," Remy said. "I gotta go get changed first."

He'd showered at Duff's. The plumbing in the trailer's bathroom hadn't worked since winter. But Remy's dad wanted to keep working the small vein he'd found while coal prices were high, and that meant the bathroom had to wait. So Remy had to catch a shower wherever he could. Lisa always said he could have shower privileges at her house, but that would mean telling her mom why. Not that he was ashamed, but Lisa's mom was a meddler. A nurse at the Dwyer Free Hospital, she knew too many social workers. One look at the trailer, and she'd have them down on Remy and his dad like hounds on a coon, signing them up for all kinds of programs. It was bad enough dodging the do-gooders at school. His dad and him didn't need any programs. They were doing okay.

Remy pulled on a clean shirt and jeans and came back out into the kitchen. His dad handed him a bowl because there weren't any clean plates, and dumped scrambled eggs into it. When Remy's dad made eggs, he put in chopped-up green and red peppers, onions, and ham when they had it. The peppers he grew himself, in a garden patch alongside the trailer. It wasn't easy to grow anything in the mountains, but Remy's dad had the touch.

"It's this mountain," he'd say. "It grew me, so I guess it can grow about anything."

They sat in quiet together while Remy ate his eggs, only the occasional rustle of the newspaper between them. It wasn't that they couldn't talk to each other, but that they knew when they could be quiet. When Remy had come back from Virginia Beach, he couldn't let himself admit he'd missed more than the mountains. He'd missed this, too.

And now sitting in the comfortable quiet with his dad, it wasn't any easier to face, the thought he'd been pushing out of his mind the past day. Summer was going by fast. If he and Lisa were going to do this—really do this—they'd have to start making plans. He'd have to tell his dad, and soon. Only now didn't seem like the right time.

"You going to the Perkinses' today?" his dad asked.

"Yeah, why?"

"There's a bag on the front porch full of eggplant and zucchini and snap beans. You drop that off at Mrs. Hambro's, all right?"

Mrs. Hambro lived next door to Lisa's parents. Her husband

had owned the Bluebird Mine. Remy's dad had a funny idea she needed to be taken care of. He didn't believe it when Remy told him she was fine. The Bluebird Mine might be played out, but Ginny Hambro had more money than anyone in McGuire County.

"Can I take the truck?" Remy asked.

"You can, but it's loaded up with coal."

Lisa'd love that, being squired around town in an old pickup full of coal.

"I thought Marty Cowell down to Hager was going to take it off my hands," his dad said, "but now he says he don't need it."

Remy looked up, tried to read his dad's face.

"You need any money?" he asked carefully. The first time he'd asked that—after he started working for Duff—his dad had about blown a hole in the roof. Later he'd explained that he didn't want Remy worrying about money. They were fine, and if they weren't, he'd find a way to fix it.

But Remy knew that mining by hand was a tough way of making money, and it worried him that his dad worked so hard. So he came up with covert ways to help, like bringing home milk and other groceries a few at a time and quietly putting them away in the cupboard.

That was something else he hadn't thought about, how his dad would manage when he was gone. They'd taken care of each other. Then again, once Remy was gone, his dad would only have himself to feed and buy clothes for, so maybe it would be easier on him. Maybe.

"Someone'll buy that coal, Remy," his dad said. "Prices are still good." He flipped the newspaper over, folded it in thirds, and used it to smack a fly on the table. "How's work going?"

"Good," Remy said. "Duff's teaching me more of the mechanical stuff. It's cool."

"Well, I know how much you like working on cars."

His dad tipped his chair back, blew smoke up toward the ceiling. The smoke hung there, a ghost of the thought in both their minds, the choice Remy'd made two years ago to stay in the high school when he could have gone to the technical school and taken the auto mechanic course. But leaving the high school would have meant leaving Lisa. They'd had a fuss about it, but Remy could be as stubborn as his dad sometimes.

Remy's dad stood and stretched. "I'm going out to work on the garden," he said.

"You are gonna put on some pants, right?"

"Yes, Remy, good lord. Don't start sounding like your mother."

"Just checking," Remy said. "You don't want to give Miss Barton a heart attack." Miss Barton was their nearest neighbor, down at the end of Walker Hollow.

"Well, if Miss Barton can see all the way up here, she deserves a good show."

Remy ended up hitching into town, catching a ride the last half of the way. He got to Bluebird Street, hoping he could dump the bag of vegetables on Mrs. Hambro's porch and run. But he wasn't that lucky. The woman had ears like an interstellar radar.

"Remy Walker!" she cried, bustling out onto the porch, her white hair twisted into a million little curls held close to her head by stiff black pins. "I haven't seen you in such a long time. You come on in here and have a cool drink."

"No, thank you, Mrs. Hambro. I can't stay. My dad asked me to give you these." He held out the plastic grocery bag full of vegetables, and Mrs. Hambro took it.

"Why, these are beautiful," she said. "Your father certainly has a gift for growing things. I do wish he'd let me give him a little something, but I don't suppose he'd accept."

"No, ma'am, he wouldn't." I would, Remy was tempted to say. I dragged the things down the mountain.

Mrs. Hambro's soft round cheeks dimpled up. "You're off to see our girl, aren't you?" She didn't have any children of her own so she'd sort of adopted Lisa and her little brother far enough to keep a nose in their business. Without losing a dimple, she said, sweet as sugar, "You'd better watch your step. I've got my eye on you."

Humming, she went back inside her house, leaving Remy stung on the front porch. He shook it off and walked to the Perkinses'.

Lisa stood at the door of the house, watching him come up the steep steps from the sidewalk, like she sensed he was coming. He never had to knock. And even though he'd seen her yesterday morning, it felt like it'd been a week. She righted everything, just by standing there. It wasn't only how pretty she was. It was that he knew her, could see the light that came from her blue eyes and feel it surround him. He ought to remember to tell her that, too.

"Hey, baby," she said.

"Hey, baby!" another voice mocked.

Scott, her ten-year-old brother, jumped out of the azaleas in front of Remy, wrapping his arms around himself and making kissing noises. Remy grabbed him and wrestled him to the ground, holding Scott's head under his arm and rubbing his hair with his knuckles.

"Who's the master?" Remy demanded.

"I am!" Scott giggled.

"Who?" Remy rubbed again.

"You are, you are!"

Remy let him go and Scott ran back behind the azaleas, shouting, "You're the master kisser! Mmmmm, mmmmm!" and shot up through the backyard, howling with laughter.

Lisa rolled her eyes and brushed a bit of grass off Remy's shoulder when he stepped up on the porch.

"The little monster," she said.

Remy leaned in to kiss her. He loved the faint scent of peaches that hung around her. It always puzzled him. He never saw any commercials on TV about any kind of shampoo or soap or anything that made you smell like peaches. It must just be her.

"You aren't babysitting, are you?"

"Only for a minute," she said. "Momma went by the store to take Daddy some lunch. She'll be back in a bit."

Lisa's dad owned the pharmacy downtown. His assistant pharmacist lived up in Beckley and wouldn't move to Dwyer, staying over the shop during the week but insisting on going home on weekends, so Mr. Perkins had to run the pharmacy himself on Saturdays. On Sundays, if someone had an emergency, he'd run and open the store.

Twining her fingers through his, Lisa led Remy into the house. The Perkinses' house was old, built back in the nineteen-twenties for a coal baron, but it was beautiful. Clean and orderly, it smelled of floor wax and furniture polish. Mrs. Perkins had a woman in twice a week to clean. Not—she said—because she minded doing it herself, but because she felt she ought to give someone the job since she could afford it.

Remy followed Lisa to the family room at the back of the house and let her pull him down on the sofa next to her. She turned and flopped on her back, her head in his lap. He looked at her, felt the quiet sense of comfort sweep over him. This was his real home, with her. She made him feel right in his world.

"What are we doing tonight?" she asked.

Remy shrugged. "Maybe we could rent a movie."

Lisa wrinkled her nose.

"Don't like that idea, huh?"

"We did that twice this week already," she said. "I think we've pretty much seen everything at the video store."

They were just biding time, Remy thought, until they could get out of here, someplace where there was more to do on a Saturday night than rent a movie.

"There isn't anything to do here," she said, but it wasn't a whine and it wasn't accusing. It was said with a hint of regret at having to admit it. "I get tired of hanging out with the same people all the time."

Remy hooked his foot over his knee and picked at the sole of his shoe and threw out the first thing that came to mind.

"We could go to a barbecue, but you'd have to get your mom's car."

He hadn't really decided if he ought to tell Lisa about Dana. But he knew she'd probably want to go to Dana's friend's cabin.

She was always up for a party. Whether he wanted to see Dana again, he wasn't sure. In a crowd of other people, maybe it would be okay.

"Who's having a barbecue?" Lisa turned to him.

"Girl I met yesterday. It's at Painter Falls Park, at one of those fancy cabins."

"Where did you meet a girl?" There was no suspicion in her eyes, face, or voice. Only curiosity.

"At the water tower."

"The *water tower*?"

"She's painting it. Painting a picture on it."

He explained about the grant and where Dana was from and how she'd come to the garage later and he'd gone with her to McDonald's. Only he left out the part about his portrait on the bag (folded up small and stuffed in an old shoe box under his bed, along with the birthday cards from his mom, a railroad spike, and a handful of trilobites).

"So she's an artist? That is so amazing. I want to meet her, Remy. Let's go," Lisa said eagerly.

A tiny squiggle of panic went up his spine, and he suddenly wished he hadn't brought it up. He didn't want to think about Dana as an amazing artist. It made her seem too interesting, more interesting than she already was.

"I don't know," he said slowly. "How about we see what Jimmy and Kayla are doing tonight? You know they got engaged?"

"I know." Lisa's pretty nose wrinkled a little. She didn't much like Kayla, Remy knew.

"Or we could hunt up Bree and Tracy and them," he offered.

They were her friends and he didn't often volunteer to spend time with them.

Her nose wrinkled further. "All they talk about anymore is clothes and guys. I swear, it's like school's over and they shut down their brains. I'm tired of them." She brushed them away with a wave of her hand. "I want to meet some new people."

I love you, Remy thought. *I love you, but I want to see her.* He felt like he'd hit a patch of ice and was swerving out of control.

"It's a haul up to Painter Falls."

"I know, but it's a great place. Some of my cousins stayed there during the family reunion a couple of years ago, and we went to see their cabin. It was so beautiful, Remy. You'll love it."

It didn't mean anything, he told himself. Not if you wanted to see a girl and talk to her. He wasn't used to it, was all. When they moved away, there'd be lots of new, interesting girls and he'd talk to them, too. It didn't mean anything.

FOUR

He knew almost right away that they shouldn't have come. It was all wrong; not just Dana, but everything—down to the park and the cabin—made him feel like he'd been yanked up out of a cool, dim place and left to squirm on the hot, hard road. The park was trim and controlled, nothing like the rambling wildness he lived next to every day, and the cabin's resemblance to a real cabin stopped at its log exterior. Near as big as Lisa's house, inside was even more luxurious. Remy'd never seen anything like it outside the TV. He had to work hard not to let it show how shriveled it made him feel. Lisa was full of how excited she was, though, all "Look at this, Remy!" and "Isn't it beautiful?" until he wanted to hug her for not caring what anyone thought of her enthusiasm.

When Dana led them through the cabin to a wide deck out back, Remy tried to find in her face or hear in her voice a clue to what they were doing, why she'd asked him and why he'd come. But Dana was different here. There might have been a flash of something in her eyes when she opened the door to let them in, but the minute Lisa started talking, it winked out. And Remy couldn't put a name to what took its place, only that it seemed like Lisa was the one Dana had invited, not him.

She took his place walking next to Lisa and Remy fell in behind them. Out on the deck, Dana introduced them with a "This is Lisa and Remy," and left them with "You'll have to figure out who everyone is."

But Lisa was good at that and Remy stuck with her for a while, until he thought it might look like he was being territorial or maybe like he couldn't function on his own. It wasn't long after he stepped away from Lisa that Dana made her way over to him.

"She's really pretty." Dana tipped her head toward where Lisa was standing, talking to a guy who said his name was Taller, but Remy couldn't be sure.

"Who is?" Remy asked, and Dana giggled.

"Um, your *girlfriend*." She handed him one of the drinks she was carrying. "Remember her?"

The cup was plastic, but it didn't look like any kind of cup he'd ever seen at a cookout. It looked like a big plastic champagne glass. There was no way to hold it and not look stupid.

"I know she is." He stared at the foggy green contents of the cup, wondered what the stuff was around the rim.

"You take that for granted?" Dana stretched out on a redwood lounge, crossing her legs and wiggling her bare toes at him. "Like you figure you deserve a pretty girlfriend?"

"I didn't say that." Remy sat on the edge of a redwood table and took a drink. Salt. It was salt on the rim. "You want me to start listing all the reasons why I know I'm lucky to have her?"

Dana smiled at him over her green drink. "You're too good to be true."

"You think?"

If he was really too good to be true, he wouldn't be here.

"You're pretty sure of her." Dana stared significantly past his shoulder and Remy turned to look.

Lisa and Taller were dancing now, Lisa leaning in close to hear something Taller said and then laughing.

"She loves to dance." Remy took another swallow, made a face, reached over, and poured the rest of his drink into Dana's cup.

"Don't you like it?"

They were so close that when Dana raised her face, he could just feel the slight warmth of her breath. Remy caught his own breath and sat back.

"Might be something you have to get used to," he said.

"Want me to get you a beer?"

"I'll get it myself."

He got up and walked over to the cooler, next to the big brick grill where Dana's friend Ian was turning long sticks with chunks of chicken and pineapple speared on them, glad for an excuse to get away from Dana.

Remy rooted through the beers, dug out a Coke, and leaned against the deck railing by the grill, under a string of fake Chinese lanterns. Smiling, Lisa looked at him over her shoulder, pointing at the Taller guy and mouthing something he couldn't understand. He nodded anyway, raised his Coke to her.

His place by Dana had been taken by some guy who didn't seem to care how stupid he looked holding a big plastic champagne glass. Dana didn't seem to mind either, laughing and hanging on him, her hand draped between his knees. Besides them, there was a glum-faced girl who alternately picked at her fingernail polish and tried to get her cell phone to work and a couple who had disappeared inside the cabin a half hour ago, making noises from an upstairs window that everyone pretended they didn't hear.

They claimed to be locals and called themselves that with a possessive boredom. The fact that they were only locals two months out of the year apparently didn't bother them. As far as Remy could tell, they picked what they wanted to be, when they wanted to be it.

"Dana says you live in Dwyer," Ian said. He was wearing a mitt on his hand printed to look like a robot claw and a West Virginia University T-shirt that said *Montani Semper Liberi*. Mountaineers are always free.

"Uh-huh."

"I bet you can't wait to get out." Ian flipped a couple of shish kebabs with his robot claw. "Where are you going to college? Marshall? WVU? Out of state somewhere?"

For a second, Remy stared at him, at his smooth tanned skin, his perfect teeth, his jeans made to look worn. Thought about how stupid it was to spend good money on jeans that were already half worn through. And what was with assuming that of course he'd want to get out? He was getting out, but still . . .

"Harvard," Remy said.

"Huh?" Ian's eyebrows shot up.

"Yeah, I'm going to Harvard." It just kind of came out, like the lie about Jarrett Mountain. He took a big swig of Coke, squinted off into the distance, contemplating his Ivy League future, while Ian stared, trying to fit Remy and Harvard together in his head.

But Remy couldn't keep from busting up.

"Yeah, right." Ian looked pissed, only a flash, then he was laughing, flipping chicken and pineapple. "So where are you going?"

Remy stopped laughing. Why couldn't he answer? Why couldn't he say "Nowhere. I'm not going to college"? It made him want to smash Ian's smooth face down on the grill with the shish kebabs.

Lisa saved him. She came to him, crossing the deck, her hips shifting unconsciously to the rhythm of music Remy'd never heard before. Her hand held out to him was like a lifeline dropped down an old mine shaft, her face the light at the top.

"I love this song!" she said, though he was sure she'd never heard it either. It wasn't her kind of music. "Come and dance with me."

He took her hand, let her pull him away from Ian and the grill, still steaming about Ian and his arrogant assumptions. He liked dancing, but the beat of this song didn't match the rolling rhythm he was used to. He modified his shuffle as best he could, watching Lisa bump and twist in front of him. She'd picked it up almost right away, taking what the other girl was doing and making it her own. He closed the gap between them, slipping his arm around her waist and moving with her.

"Where are you going?" he whispered without thinking.

"Huh?" She looked at him, not understanding.

He let her go, watched her dance, not even trying to keep up anymore, feeling his anger subside. The boy who had been talking to Dana danced between them, and Remy stepped back.

Dana stood up, her head only coming up to his shoulder, and made a little motion toward the trees.

"Wanna go for a walk?"

Remy shook his head. Maybe he didn't know why he'd come, but it wasn't for that. This was wrong. Everything here was wrong.

"I want you to help me pick up some firewood," she said.

If that was all, okay. He followed her into the trees, holding out his arms while she gathered up sticks and loaded them on him.

"Sorry you came?" she asked.

"Nope. Nothing else to do."

"So it was either us or reruns on TV."

"Something like that." He gave her a half smile. "What makes you think I'd be sorry?"

"I don't know." She broke a long stick in two. "Maybe you're not into the stuff we like to do and talk about." She laid the sticks on his pile. "You're so different."

"I'm not that different," he said. "You need to get down from your water tower and talk to more people."

"I've talked to enough." She lifted her chin. "There's something about the way you look at people. It's kind of rude, actually."

"That's pretty good, coming from you," he said. "Considering you called me scenery."

"Did I?" She laughed, trying to smother it so it came through her nose. "That was a compliment. Not like the way you look at us, like—like you think we're spoiled brats or something."

"Aren't you?"

"See?" She almost shrieked. "God, that's rude!"

"What?" Remy grinned at her. "I didn't say it. You did. I just wondered if you believed it."

"Give me those." She scrabbled the sticks out of his arms, dropping half of them and swearing.

"They're mostly no good anyway," Remy told her. "Too green."

"What's that mean?"

"Wood's got to be dry to burn. This stuff is still green. All it'll do is smoke."

"You could have said something."

Remy shrugged. "You seemed to think you knew what you were doing."

"Excuse me for not being up on my wilderness survival skills." She dumped the sticks on the ground and stood with her hands on her hips, frowning at them. "So which ones are okay?"

He helped her pick through the wood and showed her how she could tell the dry from the green. She reached for a branch and nearly jumped a mile, screaming loud enough to tear the bark off the trees.

"A snake! A huge, huge snake!"

That brought everyone else running to see, more screaming, and someone saying, "Kill it! Somebody kill it!"

"What for?" Remy asked. "Leave it alone."

Nobody listened to him. Ian went and got a shovel, but Remy stepped in front of him, picked up the stupid snake, and threw it as far as he could into the woods.

"Why'd you do that?" Ian demanded. "It'll come back."

"No, it won't," Remy said. "And even if it does, it's not going to hurt you. It's not poisonous."

"It's like you ought to have your own TV show," the noisy girl said.

"How do you know?" Dana asked.

"I just do. The only poisonous snakes around here are copperheads and rattlers. That was only an old blacksnake."

"You're a regular mountain man." Ian jammed the shovel into the ground.

"I think your pineapple is burning," Remy said.

Dana and Ian looked like they were avoiding him after that, but the rest of them seemed impressed by his casual snake-handling skills. The guys wanted to know if he rock climbed and if he knew where they could go rafting.

Lisa had disappeared. Remy looked around and saw Dana was missing, too. He found them in the living room, heads together over a sketchbook and a bunch of drawings spread out on a low table in front of them.

"So you really think you miss out on a lot not living in the dorms?" Lisa was saying.

"Well, maybe not tons." Dana closed the sketchbook. "But you make a lot of connections your first year. Living off-campus can make that hard." Dana paused, gave Lisa a long look. "So can try-ing to drag an outsider along."

Remy saw Lisa's head jerk up, startled.

"An outsider?"

"Someone who doesn't go to the college," Dana said.

Me, Remy thought with a jolt. *She's talking about me.*

"I don't think I'm all that interested in the social side anyway—" Lisa saw Remy standing in the doorway, the confusion on her face falling away. "Remy, come and look! Dana's showing me some of her drawings. Aren't they fantastic?"

But Remy couldn't move. It was the first time he'd thought of himself that way, that this time, he'd be the outsider—in more ways than one.

"Yeah. Fantastic."

"You didn't even look," Lisa said.

"Don't have time. We gotta go if you're going to get home by midnight."

Lisa went to use the bathroom and Remy leaned against the back of the sofa, waiting for her. Dana got up and came around to stand in front of him.

"What are you, her fairy godmother?"

Remy shrugged, burning. "Sounded to me like you were auditioning for the job."

"I was trying to be nice."

"Is that what you call it?" To him, it had sounded like a deliberate stab, and he wanted to stab back.

Dana stared hard at him.

"What?" Remy asked.

"I'm wondering why you even came."

"Uhhhhh . . . I was invited?"

"You know what I mean." Dana let out a huff through her nose. "I mean if all you were going to do was stand around and stare at us like we escaped from a zoo or something—I mean, what's the point?"

"I ought to ask you the same thing," he said. "Isn't that why you invited us? You found yourself some authentic hillbillies to go along with your fake cabin, and you asked us up here so you could laugh at us."

"That. Isn't. True." Dana took a deep breath. "If you weren't so defensive, people might actually get to know you."

"Maybe I don't care."

Remy looked over his shoulder, wishing Lisa would hurry up.

"You will," Dana said. "When you turn into a liability for her and she dumps you and you're stranded in some college town somewhere."

It felt like she'd punched him, and he struggled not to let it show.

"You know?" He cocked an eyebrow at her. "It almost sounds to me like you've got the hots for her."

"Oh!" she almost growled. "You're a—a—"

"A what?"

Dana was turning red, trying to think of something to call him when Lisa returned.

"What's going on?" She looked from Remy to Dana. "What are y'all talking about?"

"I don't know." Remy was trying not to crack up. "What were we talking about?"

"About how we ought to do this again sometime." Dana smiled back at him, hard.

"That'd be nice," Lisa said.

"We'd better go." Remy took hold of Lisa's elbow, then stopped and turned back to Dana. "Hey, speaking of zoos, maybe you shouldn't tell people you're a painter at Painter Falls."

"Why not?"

"Because around here, painter's another word for a mountain lion. You know, a panther. So it's really Panther Falls."

"What's that supposed to mean?" Dana asked.

Remy shrugged. "Nothing. Just thought someone ought to tell you."

"Thanks for the advice," Lisa chirped.

"No problem." Dana was still growling.

Remy and Lisa went out to where Lisa's mom's car still sat. Still because Remy'd half been expecting it to be gone or covered over with brambles or something, like the story his grandfather used to tell about the miner who was lured deep into a forgotten old shaft under the mountain by the sounds of hammers ringing like bells. There he found strange little men digging out diamonds. The men promised him a sack full of diamonds if he stayed and sang to them for a day. And so he stayed and sang every song he knew and when he was done, the men gave him a sack of diamonds so heavy he could barely carry it. It plagued him as he carried it up the shaft, pressing down on his back and bending him near double. But he wouldn't set it down. When he finally climbed out of the mine, he found that a hundred years had passed and everyone and everything he knew was gone and changed. And the sack was full of worthless coal.

Remy'd had a teacher in grade school who had loved those local stories. She told the class that their ancestors had brought them over from Europe and adapted them to their new home. What Remy could never understand about stories like that was why the little men or fairies or ogres would go to all that trouble to make someone stay with them for a hundred years. What did they get out of it?

They were quiet on the way back, Remy driving and Lisa resting against the seat, her hand on his. If she was bothered by what Dana had said about outsiders, it didn't show, while Remy sat with a hole where Dana's words had burned through. Much as he'd thrown back at her, she'd scored a direct hit.

He stopped the car at the bottom of Walker Hollow Road. Lisa sat up and looked around.

"What are you stopping here for?" she asked. "Drive on up the hollow."

He shook his head. "I don't want you to be late."

He was still confused about the party, about Ian, about Dana, and wanted to walk it off. He stopped her protest with a long kiss.

"I love you."

He climbed out of the car and watched her slide over into the driver's seat.

"You coming to church tomorrow?" she asked, fastening her seat belt. "We can come and get you."

"Yeah, okay. I'll meet you down here."

"Night, baby. Look out for bears."

"Night."

He watched as she pulled away, until the taillights were two red embers in the distance that disappeared around the curve of the mountain.

He headed up the hollow. The night was cool and there was enough of a moon to see by. A soft mist drifted down the side of the mountain and settled in the hollow like a ghost come home. Remy wasn't superstitious, didn't think there was anything in the mist but mist. All the same, it gave him a shiver to walk through it, like walking through someone's breath. The breath of the mountain.

He wished he could figure out why he felt fussed up. So Dana had changed and Ian was a smooth-faced jerk. At least Lisa'd had a good time. She'd liked how different they were, didn't matter that they were every bit as shallow as Bree and Tracy. Different was good even if it wasn't better.

Remy sighed and squinted through the darkness.

"What does it matter, anyway?"

He didn't know who he was saying it to or why he said it out loud. The only answer was the forced call of a barred owl, hoo-hoo-WHA! Like he was trying hard to laugh and couldn't get it right.

FIVE

Remy went to church usually once a month and then mainly to keep in good with Lisa's parents. It wasn't that he didn't believe in God. But the fact was, God had made so much good stuff for him to be doing, it was hard to find the time. Didn't it amount to the same thing, he wondered, if he spent a Sunday on a ramble up the mountain? After all, it was men who made the church and God who made the mountain.

In a town like Dwyer, Sunday service was the social event of the week. People came early and stayed late, standing on the gravel lot in their nice clothes and dusty shoes, fanning away the stuffy heat with a church pamphlet. The little kids ran in and out between the grownups, sometimes joined by a stray dog pretending for a little while that it belonged to someone.

It was also a chance to see what relatives were left in the county. He'd already been kissed by and had promised to go to dinner with half a dozen aunts and cousins. Now here was his mother's aunt Ina, asking if he'd heard from his mother lately.

"I never will understand what some people see in living at the beach," Aunt Ina told Remy through a cloud of flowery perfume so strong it wavered in the air between them. "Nothing but sand and sweaty tourists. You tell your mother she'll be sorry she left here someday. You tell her I said so."

"I will, Aunt Ina." What would Ina think when she found out he was going, too?

"And give my love to your daddy."

Remy bent down to let her kiss him on the cheek. His aunt Vennie took Ina's place, whipping out a tissue and vigorously rubbing off the smudge of fluorescent pink lipstick Ina'd left on Remy's cheek while she gave him a brisk rundown on which family member was in the hospital and who ought to be, but was too stubborn to admit it.

Vennie was the unofficial Walker clan secretary. She took great pride in having conquered a computer and the Internet and gloried in maintaining lists of who'd moved where and writing gossipy form letters and e-mails to keep everyone up-to-date, whether they wanted to be or not. She also organized the semiannual Walker family reunion like it was a battle and she was a four-star general.

"I haven't heard from your daddy about the reunion." She threw the words down like evidence in front of a jury. "You tell Alvin I'm coming up to talk to him about it this week. I need him to help Gary bring down chairs and fill the tubs with ice, so he better be there. You, too. July eleventh, Bantz Park. Don't you forget!"

Bantz Park. Everyone under twenty called it Pants Park, as in Take-Off-Your-Pants Park, for obvious reasons. Dark pavilions hidden under trees. Most guys Remy knew had gotten lucky there at least once. Or said they had.

Remy backed out of the crowd, trying to avoid any more elderly female relatives and looking for Lisa. At eleven-thirty, it was already steaming, the air lying over his skin like a damp, hot blanket. There'd be a storm tonight, he heard someone say. Naw, it'd follow the ridge north, someone else said. It always did when the wind come in this way. But there was no wind to speak of, only what a hundred flapping pamphlets could kick up.

The familiar lilt of their voices rolled over him, the call of neighbors, old friends, and family. Everybody knew everyone, and in between the conversation they were on the lookout, picking up new things to talk about. He caught them watching him, some of the ladies smiling because they knew who he was looking for.

There was a time it embarrassed him to be watched, but now he was used to it. He knew they did it because they were interested and they were interested because they cared. It made him feel like he was part of something.

Over his shoulder, Remy heard another conversation swell.

Didja see what's been doing to the water tower? a voice said. Painting it, a girl up there, painting pictures on the water tower. What on earth for? S'posed to bring in tourists. To look at a water tower? Well, who'da thought? Do people like looking at water towers? No way! Just another excuse, spending that senator's pork barrel money on another project won't do nobody no good.

Except for Dana, Remy thought. Dana the painter panther who didn't need any help. He didn't want to think about Dana or last night. He was feeling too good, Sunday good. He looked over the crowd, saw Jimmy and nodded at him. Kayla was hanging on his arm, flashing her ring at a bunch of girls. Jimmy telegraphed desperation, jerked his head in a "come and help me" way. Remy only laughed, shook his head.

When a state police cruiser pulled up, nobody fussed. They knew it was only Terry Hanlon stopping by to say hello.

"Hey, Remy." Terry clapped a hand on Remy's shoulder. "What you been up to? How's work going?"

Terry was Remy's mother's cousin and felt he had a sort of family duty to check up on Remy once in a while.

"Going good," Remy said. He spotted Lisa waving at him by the Perkinses' minivan.

"I take it she's waving at you, not me." Terry nodded toward Lisa.

"She better be," Remy said.

"Eh, I'm not that lucky." Terry gave Remy a little shove. "Go on. Say hey to your mom for me, next time you talk to her."

Remy made his way over to Lisa.

"You are going to come and have dinner with us?" Mrs. Perkins asked him.

"Yes, ma'am." That was the other main reason to come to church. On the weekends she wasn't working at the hospital, Mrs. Perkins always made a big, traditional Sunday dinner, the kind where you couldn't see the tabletop, there was so much food piled on it. Sometimes Remy dreamed of those dinners. "Thank you, Mrs. Perkins." It was worth laying on all the manners he could scrape up.

He climbed into the van after Lisa and spotted Miss Carter sitting on the middle-row seat too late to do anything about it.

"Hello, Remy."

Remy mumbled a "ma'am" at her.

"Miss Carter's coming to dinner, too," Lisa said, her voice apologetic.

Miss Carter taught ninth and tenth grade history with a zeal that went largely unappreciated by an audience that was more concerned with who was driving what and who was getting it on with whom than the history of the labor movement. She was one of the few McGuire County High teachers who stayed in Dwyer year-round. Mostly the teachers stayed in rooms during the school year and lit out for their own homes or other places in the summer. They hated Dwyer and the mountains and weren't there by choice, but by salary incentives used to attract new teachers to undesirable schools. Miss Carter was different. She was like a missionary whose religion was education and she spent her summers like a weekday preacher, trying to keep her flock in line until the next nine-month-long Sunday.

Remy had been a particular target of her proselytizing, exhorted to "make the most of his opportunities" and "live up to his potential" until one day two years ago when he'd lost it and told her what she could do with her grade-level requirements and earned himself a two-day suspension and a thousand-word essay on respect.

Now he slid into the backseat with Lisa and Scott, leaving Miss Carter by herself in the middle row. Mr. Perkins pulled away from the church. On the other side of Lisa, Scott leaned slightly forward and reached out a bunched-up hand toward Miss Carter's straight, slim neck in front of him. Remy lunged across Lisa, grabbed Scott's fist and pried it open, snatching up the fat green caterpillar inside.

The jostling and Scott's furious "Remy!" made Miss Carter and Mrs. Perkins turn around to look.

"Boys!" Mrs. Perkins commented in general, rolling her eyes. And Miss Carter laughed but gave Remy a look. Miss Carter didn't miss much, but Remy wasn't giving anything away, so he had to sit with the spiny, squirming caterpillar in his hand until they got to the Perkinses' house.

"You're such a wiener!" Scott said when they got out of the van.

Remy dropped the caterpillar down the back of his shirt, sending Scott squealing up the bank.

Dinner was two golden, roasted chickens with sage stuffing, mashed potatoes, gravy, biscuits, creamed corn, spiced apples, and a dish of Mrs. Perkins's own pickled ramps—wild leeks that grew in the mountains, though most people didn't eat them anymore.

"Ramps!" Miss Carter exclaimed over them.

"You know, I don't feel right if I don't put some up every year, the way my grandmother used to," Mrs. Perkins said. "It's a real shame how that tradition is dying out. There used to be a ramp festival in the spring here when I was a girl."

"Isn't it funny how things change?" Miss Carter asked. "A friend of mine in New York tells me that ramps are a delicacy in some of the best restaurants there."

"Well, down here, they used to be a necessity," Mr. Perkins said. "First green thing folks had to eat since before winter. They'd eat so much, they'd start to smell. My daddy remembered school being closed down for days during ramp season because the kids smelled so bad!"

"Cool!" Scott said.

"Don't get any ideas." Miss Carter waved her fork at him. "Or I'll make sure the entire staff of the elementary school is supplied with gas masks."

Under the table, Remy felt Lisa's foot find his, and he forgot about Miss Carter and the ramps.

"I think they're disgusting," Lisa said, her toes sneaking up under the cuff of Remy's pants. "I don't know why you bother with them, Momma."

"See?" Mrs. Perkins said to Miss Carter. "No appreciation for her heritage."

"You wait until you've lived somewhere else for ten years and can't get any," Miss Carter said. "Then you'll appreciate them."

"There might be some things I'll miss," Lisa said. "But ramps won't be one of them."

"I'm sure there'll be plenty of things you'll miss," Miss Carter said. "So you're going to Dickinson College? That's in Pennsylvania, am I correct?"

Remy's muscles seemed to seize up on him and he sat, a fork loaded with potatoes and gravy dripping over his plate, frozen by Miss Carter and her nosy questions. He didn't know where they would lead, didn't know if Lisa'd told her parents about their plans. And somehow didn't want it coming up now, cutting through the butter-soft day like a hot knife.

"Momma and Daddy wanted me to go to WVU, of course," Lisa said, "but I wanted to go out of state."

"Now, we told you it's up to you," Mr. Perkins said.

West Virginia University was in Morgantown, hundreds of miles away, which in the mountains was as good as thousands. Even if Lisa'd decided to go there, it wouldn't have made a differ-

61

ence, it was so far away. Remy forced his arm to push the potatoes into his mouth.

"After I graduate from college, I'd like to go somewhere really different, like New York, maybe. Or out west," Lisa said.

The potatoes felt like a mouthful of dry dirt. Remy choked them down. New York? She'd never said a word about New York before. Or maybe she had and he hadn't heard her. He couldn't remember. But now here she was talking about going to New York and he could hardly move.

"*I'm* going to West Virginia University," Scott said around a wad of biscuit, breaking Remy's stone spell. "Gonna play football."

"You better bulk up a little first, shorty," Remy said, forcing his voice to sound normal.

Scott opened his mouth wide in Remy's direction, giving him a clear view of half-chewed biscuit.

"Scott!" Mrs. Perkins scolded.

"I think it's a good idea to take advantage of any opportunity to see as much of the world as possible." Miss Carter was carefully cutting a piece of chicken, but her eye was on Remy as she spoke. "There is so much outside these mountains that you can't know unless you get out there and experience it."

Remy considered following Scott's example, but didn't want to embarrass Mrs. Perkins.

"You can always come back," Miss Carter continued. "Like your parents."

"Well, it was different for us," Mr. Perkins said. "I had my father's business to take over, though business has been dwindling steadily." He smiled privately. "Besides, Lisa isn't interested in being a pharmacist, are you, honey?"

What was she interested in? *What was she interested in?* Remy felt panicked, like it was a one-question final and everything depended on it. How could he not know?

"Speaking of the pharmacy . . ." Mr. Perkins wiped his mouth on a napkin and stood. "I promised Miss Laidlaw I'd open up for her this afternoon, so I'd better get down there. Pleasure to see you again, Miss Carter."

"I better go, too," Remy said after Mr. Perkins had gone. "I told Duff I'd help him out this afternoon so he could go see his grandma."

It was a lie. He didn't really have to go, but he was shaken by New York and the idea that he had no clue what Lisa wanted to study in school. He felt like she had taken a step away from him and he'd have to run to catch up. What else didn't he know? Stuff that would make him a liability, like Dana had said. And he couldn't sit there and listen to Miss Carter witness for the outside world anymore. He pushed his chair back.

"Remy." Lisa's voice was questioning, tinged with a bit of hurt. "I didn't know you were working today."

"I forgot," Remy said. "I'm sorry. My schedule's all crazy this summer, filling in for people." It was true. Just not today.

"You're still working at the gas station?" Miss Carter asked the way she might have asked him if he was cleaning outhouses for Satan.

"Well, it only looks like a gas station from the outside," Remy said. "It's really a front for an international spy ring."

Scott snorted milk through his nose.

"I'm serious. You remember when all those people reported seeing a plane come down over on Deer Ridge, but they never

63

found a trace of it? Well, that was one of ours. Experimental hover-craft. The cloaking device malfunctioned."

"What a load of crap!" Scott shouted.

"*Scott!*" Both Mrs. Perkins and Lisa said it at the same time.

"Thanks for dinner, Mrs. Perkins," Remy said. "It was great, as usual."

From the front porch of the Perkinses' house, the town looked small, a jumble of buildings in the bottom. Growing up in the sparse settlement of Walker Hollow, Remy had always seen Dwyer as a destination, a place to be, but he'd outgrown that feeling. There was a whole lot more than just Dwyer and Walker Hollow, he knew that. But the way Miss Carter said it, she didn't really mean more, she meant everything worthwhile. It was of a piece with what Ian had said. "I bet you can't wait to get out." Like Dwyer was some kind of a pit to climb out of.

He walked through town, down the minicanyon of Main Street, the sun angled in front of him giving everything an orange glow. It made everything look gold, but Remy knew his town, like he knew his trailer and the way he and his father lived. It wasn't gold.

Even back in the coal boom when these buildings went up—the hotels, the offices, the courthouse with the stone eagles out front—it wasn't gold then, either. It was built up to bring in strong backs to dig out the coal. Now the coal was gone and the buildings were empty, the hotels and offices were boarded up, paint was peeling on the old miners' houses, and the kudzu that had crawled out of the river crept over everything. Dwyer was old and worn out, past the purpose it was built for.

Remy saw all of that, but he also saw how carefully Mr. Perkins kept up the outside of his store, same as his father had kept it fifty years ago, the gold lettering shining on the window. Saw on every corner the half barrels full of flowers the Baptist ladies tended. Saw Amy Cameron taking in old Mr. Darrow's laundry for him. He saw how he knew almost everyone he passed and they knew him. People Miss Carter would probably say hadn't realized their potential.

Behind him, the sounds of hammers and saws rang out into the street from the library. Usually closed on Sundays, it was open now for the volunteers, still cleaning up from the bad flooding back in May that had damaged the carpet and the shelves and wiped out hundreds of books, piled in a damp and broken heap in the parking lot. The double doors were propped open to the air, carrying out sawdust and voices talking, laughing, someone picking on a guitar.

Remy walked over to the library, stuck his head in the door. Most everyone recognized him, stopped what they were doing to wave tools at him. And suddenly the thought of swinging a hammer for an hour or two—with people who knew him and welcomed him—sounded pretty appealing.

"Can you use an extra pair of hands?" he asked.

For the rest of the afternoon, he hammered nails into boards, building shelves for new books, for a town full of people who didn't know they were living in a time warp, people who'd been left behind or were too stupid to get up and go.

Everywhere else in that great big world Miss Carter was so hung up on, everything was growing. Remy knew because he saw it on TV. Suburban sprawl, they called it sometimes. Parts of the cities might die, but towns didn't. They grew and spread. They didn't dry up like a pool of water that lost its source. Was Dwyer drying up? Its people were evaporating. Did they feel the pull of the atmosphere, drawing them away? Is that what Lisa felt? Remy wasn't sure if he felt it at all.

Maybe he wasn't water. Maybe he was stone. Was it so wrong to be a stone?

S I X

Mondays were Duff's day off. Jimmy was supposed to take over at six a.m. with Remy coming in at eight. But when Remy got to the garage, Ron the night-shift guy was still there and as mad as a wet cat.

"Second time in a week Reynolds been late. I don't mind a half hour here and there, but two hours! I got a kid at home and a wife who's got to get to work. Duff's gonna hear about it."

"C'mon, Ron," Remy said. "Jimmy'll make it up to you."

"Uh-uh. Not this time. I'm sick of covering his ass."

Ron tossed the cash register keys at Remy and left.

Business was heavy, as usual for a Monday. That's why it took two of them to handle it. Remy considered calling Matt or one of the part-time guys to come and help, but there wasn't even time for that. There were three oil changes scheduled to be done by that afternoon, Jimmy's usual job. If they didn't get done, Duff'd lose business. Remy pulled the first car up on the ramp and tried to work on it, but with the pump traffic interrupting, it took him near two hours. And Jimmy still hadn't shown up.

There was no time for lunch—and no one to cover for him anyway. Remy ate a couple of packs of saltine crackers from the bowl next to the coffeemaker and went back to work on the second car, but he couldn't find the right oil filter and spent twenty minutes tearing up the storeroom looking for one. When he came back out, he saw that someone had taken five bottles of 10W-40 from the rack outside the office.

He was so mad, he kicked the rack as hard as he could, knocking it over and sending the rest of the bottles tumbling down the bank and into the creek.

That brought out every royal blue cussword he could think of as he slid down the bank on his backside, gathered the bottles out of the creek, and threw them back up on top of the bank. He was still swearing as he climbed out, a bottle of oil in each hand, and saw Lisa standing there.

"Hey," was the best he could manage.

"Hey yourself." She stood with her hands on her hips, looking him up and down like a detective eyeing a suspect. "What's going on?"

Something was up. He could hear it in her voice and the way she stood there. He wasn't in the mood to hear it.

"You want to help me pick these up?" he asked her. Better turn the mind to the job in front of him.

Lisa righted the oil rack, helped him wipe the mud off the bottles and put them back on the rack.

"What happened?" she asked.

"Jimmy never showed up this morning. Ron's mad as hell and

is going to tell Duff. I got two more oil changes to do and people coming in like there's a gas shortage and then someone steals five bottles of oil while I'm back in the storeroom. I'm gonna kill Jimmy if he doesn't get in here soon."

Remy waited for her to say something soothing, to pity him. But she only stood with her arms crossed, staring across the road at the dollar store, waiting for him to ask the obvious.

Not yet. He didn't need another problem right then.

"Can you watch things here for a minute?"

"Hmm?" She turned and looked at him like she hadn't heard.

"I've gotta go to the can. Can you keep an eye on things? Make sure somebody doesn't walk off with a pump?"

"Sure."

She was pissed, all right. It was that kind of day, everything going wrong. In the bathroom, Remy splashed cold water over his face and the back of his neck. He was steaming, sweaty with heat and frustration. He rubbed himself dry with a coarse paper towel until his skin tingled, leaving him feeling a little better.

Back out front, there were more customers waiting. He pumped gas, checked oil, and cleaned windshields, conscious the whole time of Lisa leaning against the wall, examining her fingernails.

"I've got to work on this car," he said when they were alone. "Come and talk to me."

She followed him into the garage and leaned against the workbench while he slid under the car.

"So what's wrong? I mean, I can see you're mad. You don't have to draw me a picture."

"If you don't have time to talk to me," she said, "I can just go."

"Come on, Lisa." He tried to loosen the plug on the oil pan, banged his knuckles on the wrench, and swore. "I'm not having the best day here."

Remy heard her sigh, saw her shift her weight on her feet.

"You lied to me yesterday."

She didn't sound angry. She sounded like she was going to cry. He swore again.

"I came by last night and you weren't here." Lisa sniffed. "Duff was here and said he hadn't seen you because it was your day off. Your day off, Remy!" She was rolling now. "I thought you were going to be with me yesterday, but you made up a lie so you didn't have to and I want to know where you went and why it was so important."

"Lisa, I—" The plug came loose all of a sudden. "Damn! Shoot that pan under here for me, would you?"

He fumbled for the pan and positioned it to catch the oil, then crawled out from under the car and stood, wiping the oil off his hands with a rag. He concentrated hard, rubbing carefully around his fingernails, as though they weren't already pretty much permanently stained black. Working at the library—physical work, hammering and carrying—he'd been able to push away the trouble brought up yesterday with Miss Carter. But Lisa was still standing there, waiting for an explanation. How could he make her understand what he didn't understand himself?

His eyes rose slowly from his fingernails to Lisa. She stood waiting, her face caught between anger and hurt. He couldn't lie.

"I went to the library and helped them fix up from the flood."

"So you just get up from dinner and go help out at the library and don't tell me?"

"I had some thinking to do," he said.

"About what?"

"About you." She looked scared, and he hurried on to tell her, "And me. About us leaving here when you go to college." He picked up his wrenches and wiped them carefully too, before putting them on the workbench. "Do you think about it? I mean *really* think about it?"

"Of course I do." Lisa ran her fingers down his arm.

Remy turned and looked at her again, his eyes holding hers. "What do you think?"

"That I want to go to college. I'm going to college." Her eyes and her voice were very steady, very sure. "And you're coming with me."

"I know. I know we've talked about that." He looked at the winch and pulley system in the roof of the garage. "But we never talked about New York. I don't want to go to New York."

She dismissed that with a wave. "I just said that for the heck of it. I'm not going to New York, either."

"But do you ever think about what it's going to mean to leave here?"

"I wish I knew what was going on with you." Lisa sighed a little, not answering his question. "We've been talking about this forever. Now it's going to happen. How many people get to make their dreams come true like that?"

Maybe that was it. Maybe it was too scary to have a dream come true. You had to pay for that somehow, sometime.

"Look—" Lisa put her hand on his forearm. "You're going to come with me. You'll get a job. We'll get a little apartment. It's what I've always dreamed about, for us to be together, on our own." She

71

reached up his arm, around his neck. "I know it's scary to leave here, but it'll be okay. Don't worry anymore, baby. We'll be together. We'll take care of each other."

He wanted to ask her about what Dana said, about dorms and outsiders and liabilities, but she put her fingers over his lips.

"I couldn't stand to think of leaving here without you," she said. "I need you to be with me."

She kissed him and he felt the familiar sensation of melting into her. It made him believe it would be good because it always had been with her. He had to have faith in what they had. He pulled her close in spite of the grease and grime. Whatever he had to pay, Lisa was worth it.

She went on home after he promised to stop by when he was done working. Duff showed up, complaining about Jimmy.

"Give him a chance to explain," Remy said. "Maybe something happened."

"Could be," Duff said. "But I'm running a business here, Remy, not a nursery school. You done with this car?"

"Nearly," Remy said.

"Finish up and you can go on home."

Remy finished the oil change and dropped the hood on the car, running his rag over it, wiping up any smudges he'd left. Then he picked up the pan of old oil and poured it into a big collection drum. He took off his coveralls and hung them on a peg in the storeroom, scrubbed his hands good in the bathroom, and went to say goodbye to Duff.

"Duff?" Remy stood in the office doorway. "You ever think of leaving here? Going to live somewhere else?"

"I've already been somewhere else." Duff leaned back in his

chair. "I spent three years in the army. I've been to Germany, Turkey, Afghanistan, and even New Hampshire. I saw enough to know where I belong."

You can always come back, Miss Carter had said.

"So you think it's a good idea to go see the world some?"

Duff rocked in the chair. "I think it's a good idea to know your mind, whatever that takes."

Remy looked at his shoes, his shoulders slumping.

"I also think"—Duff squinted at him—"it's a good idea to know if you're thinking with your mind or some other part of your anatomy."

"It isn't just that with Lisa." Remy picked up a nail from Duff's desk and ran it around the edges of his fingernails, trying to dig out the thick oil and grime.

"Yeah, well . . ." Duff stretched his arms over his head. "It ain't always easy to tell. But look, Remy, anyone can see you got something on your mind. You been unsettled for a week, and now you're asking questions about getting out and seeing the world. That what's going on here? You and Lisa planning to go out and see the world?"

Remy concentrated on the grime. "She's going to college, and I'm going with her." Funny how simple the words sounded.

"You're going to college?" Duff asked.

Okay, so it wasn't that simple. Remy explained their plans.

"Huh," Duff said. "What's your daddy think about it?"

Remy shrugged. "Haven't told him yet."

It nagged at him, without Duff reminding him. There was a look he'd seen in his dad's eyes when his mom had gone, and another look he'd seen the day his dad came to get him at Virginia

Beach, two closely related looks and both speaking of pain Remy'd never known. He didn't want to be the one responsible for bringing such a look to his dad's eyes again.

"Well," Duff said. "Sounds like a plan. Might've been better if you'd gone to the tech school and got your auto mechanic certification. But I guess those plans weren't as important, huh?"

Remy rammed the point of the nail under his skin. Swearing, he dropped the nail and put his finger to his mouth to suck the wound, the taste of blood and engine grease mixing.

"Sometimes you are so daggoned dumb." Duff bent over and picked up the nail. "Go on home."

Remy left the garage on foot and didn't go to Lisa's house, even though he knew that both of her parents were working and they'd have the house to themselves. Instead, he walked up the mountain along Highway 25, the curve of the road following the curve of the land, making a kind of order he could understand. He walked fast, his hands jammed in his pockets, his mind aboil with that technical school mess.

Even though it was two years ago, it still stung. The mechanic certification course was a big deal. You didn't just sign up for it. You had to pass a tough test, and he'd scored highest in the county. He'd only been going out with Lisa a few months and was planning to show her his results, all jacked up about it. Then it hit him that it'd mean leaving her and maybe losing her. The technical school was way over in Felter and it'd mean not seeing her at all during the week.

He'd tried thinking toward the future, how much money he could make with that certification under his belt, how he could take her places and buy her things. But it wouldn't be the same, not being in the same school, not being with her every day.

So he didn't go, sent back his acceptance packet without filling out any of the forms.

The blaring of a car horn made him nearly jump off the side of the mountain. He turned to yell at the driver, but the car had screeched to a stop and Jimmy leaned out, shouting.

"Hey, boy! I been looking for you. Gotta tell you something!"

Remy walked over and leaned on the window frame. "Where you been? You know Duff's not too happy about you not showing up for work today."

"I don't care." Jimmy grinned wide enough to split his face. "Get in. We got some celebrating to do."

"Celebrating what?" Remy flattened himself against the car as another car swept by.

"I'm leaving, getting out of here. I'll tell you all about it. Just get in before you get killed."

Remy climbed into the car and Jimmy pulled off.

SEVEN

Where are you going, Jimmy?"

"We're gonna go have some fun!" Jimmy cranked up the radio.

"No!" Remy shouted over Garth Brooks singing about having friends in low places. "You said you were leaving. Leaving to go where? Where were you today?"

"I had a job interview over in Barlow." Jimmy swept up Highway 25, past the water tower.

"Barlow?" Remy asked. "Where's that?"

"It's over in Virginia. They got a factory there where they make carpet. Kayla's uncle got me the interview. I got the job, Remy. Kayla and me are leaving the end of the week to find an apartment."

"Jesus." Remy stared out the window. Jimmy was leaving. Just like that. "How come you never said anything before?"

"About what?"

"About this job."

"Didn't know about it till Sunday. It come up all of a sudden."

It sure had.

"What kind of work is it?"

Jimmy stared at him, like he couldn't figure out why anyone would ask. "I don't know. It's a job in a factory. You run some big machine."

"Is it good pay?"

"Yeah! Well, more'n I make at Duff's."

"But you won't know anybody in Barlow."

"Not right off." Jimmy stared again, his brows coming together. Then he cracked a big grin and smacked Remy in the chest. "I'll worry about that later. Right now, we're celebrating!"

Remy had to think for a second to figure out what they were celebrating, when it was really the first of the goodbyes you'd have to say if you were leaving. But Jimmy was only doing what Remy was going to do in a month and a half. Going on, making a life. That ought to deserve a celebration.

"Well . . . okay. Let's do it!" Remy shoved some quick enthusiasm into his voice.

Jimmy drove up the highway to Ferguson's, a bar along the river. They were both of them underage, but that didn't slow Jimmy down. Remy hesitated a second at the door, in the red and blue glow of the neon sign.

"I can't go in there, Jimmy."

"Ain't nobody going to care," Jimmy said. "We're only going to have a beer, play pool, maybe dance with some girls. Come on. I'm entitled."

Suddenly, it seemed like the right way to end the whole rotten day, so Remy followed Jimmy through the door. Inside, warm air, smoke, music, deep voices, and the heady smell of beer wrapped around him, thick enough to swim through almost, making him feel buzzed before he'd even had a drink.

At the bar, a couple of men knew them, and Remy figured they were busted already.

"Your daddy know you're in here, boy?" Dave, a big guy in a union cap, said to Remy.

But when they heard Jimmy's news, they seemed to think it was party-worthy, going "Woo hoo!" and clapping Jimmy on the back.

"What are you drinking?" Dave asked. "This round's on me."

"You got the right idea," his friend Harold said to Jimmy. "Now's the time to get out, while you're young and can get a good start."

They sat at a table and the barmaid came over with a tray of beers.

"You're smart," Harold said to Jimmy. "I wish I'da been that smart when I was your age."

"Hell," Dave said, "you don't have to be a rocket scientist to see ain't nobody making a fortune living in these mountains."

"Wouldn't there be anything you'd miss, though?" Remy asked over his beer.

"Well, let me think." Dave rubbed his chin. "We got one of the lowest crime rates in the country."

"Only because nobody has anything worth stealing," Harold said.

And they busted up laughing. It was an old joke, so old it had hair on it, made funnier because it was true and because most people didn't care that it was. What it really meant was they were all pretty much equal.

Remy downed the rest of his beer, and Dave went to the bar and brought back another round. A couple more guys joined them and it turned into a celebration of running down West Virginia and the mountains.

"How come ducks fly over West Virginia upside down? 'Cause there's nothing worth crapping on!"

"What's the difference between a hillbilly wedding and a hillbilly funeral? One less drunk at the funeral!"

Same old stuff Remy'd heard before, most of his life. Underneath it all, you could hear the affection, could tell they didn't really mean what they were saying. Only now Remy felt like he was watching them from outside, through the wavy glass bottom of his beer mug, and what they were saying struck him as being more true than funny, and he wondered how they could laugh at it.

The barmaid brought another round, and Remy gulped his beer, hoping it'd make what everyone was saying sound funny, instead of making him want to hit someone.

"What's the matter with you?" Dave asked. "You look like someone peed in your beer."

"It's not funny, what you're saying," Remy said.

"Everyone's a critic," Harold said.

"No, listen." Remy waved his beer at them. "If you keep telling those jokes, it just helps keep those ideas going."

"Whatever." Dave emptied his mug.

"That's how that stuff gets around," Remy insisted. "And then everyone believes it's true. Don't you think?"

"I think you need to lighten up," Harold said. "Hey, Jimmy! Do something about your friend."

"What?" Jimmy yelled. "Wait a sec."

Jimmy got up and tried to walk around the table, but stumbled and fell against a big truck driver. The truck driver gave Jimmy a shove, and Jimmy swore at him.

"Maybe you boys ought to go home," the barmaid said. "You ain't driving, are you?"

"Come on, give me the keys." Dave held out his hand, but Jimmy smacked it away, and that's when the whole place went crazy, like in a movie, a real live barroom brawl, with fists flying and people falling over each other.

Remy sat and watched it like he was seeing it through that same thick glass, like it wasn't real.

"You better get out the back way, boy, before the police come," Harold told him. "The McGuire County detachment office ain't even a mile down the road. They'll be here any second."

What did that have to do with him? Remy wondered. It was Jimmy who was fighting. Then it hit him that he could get run in for underage drinking and realized Harold was right. He needed to get out of there. Only he couldn't seem to figure out where the door was. Everywhere he turned, there was another tangle of bodies, and he stumbled, trying to step over them. Harold caught him by the elbow and pulled him up.

But by then it was too late. The lights of police cars flashed through the front windows, and the next thing Remy knew he was sitting in the back of a state police cruiser.

I trust you not to be dumb enough to get into trouble, his dad had told him. Well, he was in trouble now. His head flopped back on the cruiser's seat.

"How old are you, Remy?" the trooper asked.

Remy lifted his head with an effort and peered into the front of the cruiser.

"Jesus, Remy, are you so drunk you don't recognize me?"

"Terry?" Great. It was Terry Hanlon, his mother's cousin and about as straight as they come. This was going to be brutal. Remy flopped back on the seat again.

He must've passed out. When he opened his eyes, the cruiser had stopped and Terry was hauling him out by his shirt.

"C'mon, Remy. I ain't carrying you."

No, he didn't want to be carried into the police station, either. He straightened up and looked around, but he didn't see the station, only a light coming from the window of a trailer. His trailer.

Terry put an arm around him and helped him stumble up the steps of the wooden porch Remy and his dad had built, and banged on the door. After a couple of minutes, Remy's dad opened the door and stood there in boxers and a T-shirt, scratching himself and yawning.

"Evening, Alvin," Terry said. "I pulled Remy out of a big bust-up over at Ferguson's. He's pretty drunk, but as far as I know, he hasn't been in any trouble before. I figured you'd see to it he doesn't get in any more after this."

Remy's dad swore. "I appreciate it, Terry. I didn't think he was stupid enough to go get drunk in a bar. Bring him on in." His dad stepped back, but Remy put his hand against the doorframe.

"Wait!" Remy stumbled back down the steps, fell on his face in the dirt, and threw up.

"Well, at least he had the sense to do it outside," his dad said. He helped Terry haul Remy into the trailer and drop him facedown on the sofa.

Remy heard them mumbling together by the door, but couldn't make out what they were saying over the roaring in his ears. He moaned and buried his face in the old blanket that covered the sofa, waiting for his dad to ream him out. But his dad only draped a quilt over Remy, turned out the lights, and went to his own bed.

Remy lay in the dark, feeling like the whole trailer was sliding down the hill, his head pounding and his stomach twisted. It had been one hell of a day.

EIGHT

He woke to the sound of people screaming at each other in Japanese. Or maybe he wasn't hearing right, maybe he'd damaged his eardrums last night. Who knew? But no, he opened his eyes a crack and saw his dad sitting in the armchair, watching a Japanese game show on satellite and eating a breakfast burrito. They didn't have a phone, but they had satellite TV. It was all about priorities.

Remy pushed himself up on the sofa, and right away wished he hadn't. Real easy, he lowered himself back down and closed his eyes. The smell of the burrito crawled up his nostrils and set his stomach rolling. Remy moaned and put a hand over his face.

"Hang in there," his dad said. "I got something for you. Meantime, there's a bucket on the floor, just in case." He went to the kitchen and came back with a glass full of brown liquid.

"What is it?" Remy peered through his fingers.

"It's Coke," his dad said. "I let it sit out so it'd go flat."

"Ohhhhhh!" Remy moaned again. "I can't drink that."

"Well, it's this or a prairie oyster."

"What's that?"

"Raw egg and Worcestershire sauce."

"Aw, Dad, c'mon!" Remy turned to face the back of the sofa and pulled the blanket up to his chin. "Can't you bring me a glass of water and leave me alone?"

"You know, you ain't exactly in a position to be giving orders here, especially considering how you got home last night and the condition you were in. The last thing I need is the Hanlons coming down on me for how bad a job I'm doing raising their kin."

"You're not doing a bad job," Remy mumbled into the cushions. "I mean, I'm almost eighteen and that's the first time I've ever been drunk."

"Well, it ain't like you broke a local record, Remy!" His dad banged a glass of water down on the table next to the sofa. "You were lucky it was Terry pulled you out of that place, otherwise you know where we'd be this morning? We'd be standing up in juvenile court."

Remy twisted his head to look at his dad all fired up. He laughed, imagining him in court.

"You think it's funny, but I ain't gonna have no one messing with me like that, I'm telling you right now. I got you this far. You got two months to go until you turn eighteen and then you can go out and screw up all you want."

His dad flopped back down in the armchair and started flicking through TV channels. Remy sat up and watched him, the crease between his dad's eyebrows deepening with each channel that passed.

"I'm sorry," Remy said. "I guess I wasn't thinking."

"Don't give me that, either," his dad said without looking away from the screen. "Like you don't have a brain of your own, like space aliens took control of you and forced you to go into Ferguson's and get tanked."

Remy laughed again. "You've been watching too much TV, Dad."

"So what, then? You just stopped thinking, walked into Ferguson's, and started drinking?"

Remy stopped laughing. "No."

"Then what the hell were you doing in a bar, son?" His dad slammed the remote on the coffee table. "When I tell you I trust you to be smart, I mean that as a compliment. I never cracked down on you because I never felt like I had to. Maybe that was wrong."

"It wasn't wrong."

"Then what were you doing in that bar?"

"It was Jimmy." Remy pulled his knees up and leaned on them. "Jimmy's leaving Dwyer. He's moving to Virginia to go work in a carpet factory. He wanted to celebrate."

Remy's dad snorted. "Well, that's something to celebrate, ain't it? A lifetime of making carpet. That Jimmy's dream in life?"

As far as Remy could tell, Jimmy's dream was to have a good time as often as possible. But you had to live, and it took money to live.

"Jimmy's getting married," Remy said. "He's got to think about that, about making more money. What's it matter if he's making carpet or fixing cars?"

"Nothing, I guess," his dad said, "except he'll be making carpet in Virginia."

"What's wrong with Virginia?"

"Nothing," Remy's dad said again. "To some people, it don't matter where they live."

Remy frowned. Now was the time.

"Sometimes it's more than that," he said.

"What's more than what?"

"Why people go." The words came carefully, with a soft precision. "It isn't that they don't care where they live, but there's something else they want."

"Oh yeah?" His dad said. "And what's Jimmy want out in Virginia?"

"I'm not talking about Jimmy." Remy took a breath. "I'm talking about me."

He waited, but his dad didn't say anything, only looked at Remy, his eyes narrowing a little. Remy had to keep going, dump the rest of it out.

"I'm leaving, too." It wasn't the way he meant to say it. The words were too scalpel accurate. "In September, when Lisa leaves for college. I'm going with her."

He waited again, just for a beat, but his dad kept quiet.

"I mean, I'm not going to college, but I'm going to go live with her. In an apartment. I'll get a job and work while she's at school. I'm real good with cars, you know that. Duff'll give me a good reference. And maybe, I don't know, maybe I can get my mechanic's certification before too long." He was rambling now, saying those things that had been churning in his mind all week. He took another breath because it was done now. But still his dad didn't say anything.

"I love her, Dad," Remy said. "I want to be with her."

More than I want to be here. More than I want to be with you. Remy took in the truth of what he was saying, like taking a knife to himself.

His dad rubbed a hand over his face and sat, staring at the TV.

"Well," he said at last. "That's something, all right. That's a reason." His fingers crept slowly along his jawline. "So, when did you come up with this idea?"

"We've been talking about it for a while. Since last year, when Lisa knew where she was going for college. But we didn't really decide until last week."

"What do her parents think of this?"

They think it's great. They're behind us a hundred percent, he thought of saying. But it wasn't true. What was true was . . .

"I don't know. I don't know if she told them yet."

"What else don't you know?" His dad got up from his chair. "Don't you know you'll only be eighteen in September, when you're planning on getting out of here? You're gonna have a heck of a time finding someone to give a lease to an eighteen-year-old kid who ain't got no credit references." He stopped in front of Remy. "And what are you gonna live on until you find this job you're talking about?"

"I don't know," Remy said again. He couldn't think, his head feeling like his brain was trying to kick its way out. "I have some money."

In the South Mountain Bank, he had over a thousand dollars squirreled away. Money for a car, he'd always planned.

"A thousand dollars ain't gonna last you long, Remy," his dad said. "And I thought you were saving up for a car. What are you going to do—how are you going to get to this job you're hoping to find without a car—wherever it is you're going? Where are you going, anyway?"

"Pennsylvania." Remy didn't want to look at his dad's face, couldn't think about how he was feeling. But Remy had to start his own life. His dad would get used to the idea. It wasn't like Remy expected him to be happy about it. It'd be worse if he said "Sure! Go! Have a nice life. I don't care."

His dad sat down on the coffee table and turned his head away. Then stood up again, shifting his weight from one foot to the other like the floor was hot.

"You're too young!" he shouted. "Too young to make a decision like this without talking to anybody. It *ain't* a good enough reason at your age! You probably won't listen to anything I could tell you anyway. You think you know everything. I know. I was there, too. We all been there. But Jesus God, Remy . . ."

His dad's voice cut off, like a fist had tightened around his throat. He ran his hands through his dark hair and stared at the ceiling.

"I know what I want," Remy muttered.

That brought his dad's eyes back down from the ceiling.

"And you think that ain't ever going to change," his dad said. "Don't you think everyone who's ever been in love has thought that? And a whole awful lot of them have been wrong."

Like you, Remy thought. *Like Mom*. But that had to be different. Otherwise, one of them would have made the choice he was making. Choose a person over a place.

"You talk to your mom about this?" His dad looked at him sideways.

Remy shook his head. "Not yet."

His dad sighed. "I want you to think, son. Think long and hard before you make any plans that can't be unmade."

"I been thinking," Remy mumbled.

"Okay, look. Please just . . ." But his voice broke again, and he shook his head. "I gotta go. I'm fixing old Mr. Herman's porch today."

He stomped to the kitchen, grabbed his trucker cap from the counter, and jammed it on his head.

"Anyway," his dad said, his back to Remy, "this don't excuse you for being stupid and getting drunk, especially for being stupid enough to get caught. While you're living here, I'm still responsible for you and I want you home by eleven from now on. Every night. You got me?"

"All right."

Remy couldn't take any more and fell back onto the pillow, turning his face against the back of the sofa, listening to the screen door slam as his dad left. He must've fallen asleep; when he woke up, his dad was gone and a woman with a thin, reedy voice was singing on the TV. Remy didn't understand the words she was singing, but her voice felt like something—something he knew. That reaching ache you sometimes heard in bluegrass music that had come to the mountains in the folk songs of the first settlers, an inheritance that traveled down over him and twisted itself around his heart. He got up and turned off the TV.

In the kitchen, he moved some dishes from the sink so he could wash himself. Water dripping from his face, he leaned on the counter and peered out the window over the sink at the neat rows of vegetables in his dad's garden. Had Jimmy been arrested last night? He wondered if Terry would tell him if he went down to the station. Kayla'd be furious. Getting arrested cost money and Kayla was sharp about money.

Whatever his dad said, Remy knew he and Lisa had something better, stronger. And that made his leaving different. He was going to be with Lisa. Nothing else could feel like this, no matter how old you were. It wasn't about sex. It was about knowing someone as much as you knew yourself, about caring . . .

Damn. He'd forgotten, totally forgotten that he'd promised to stop by her house last night.

Remy pushed away from the sink. He had to find her and talk to her.

Lisa was not happy.

"I'm getting a little tired of you forgetting about me."

They were sitting on the old stone wall at the bottom of the slope of her parents' front yard.

"You're lucky you weren't arrested," she said.

"Yeah, lucky I'm related to half the police force." He propped his shoulder against hers. "I told my dad."

It was still raw. An open wound.

"About what?"

"About us, leaving." He let out a short laugh. "Seems like a lot of people talking about leaving lately."

"Why would anyone talk about staying?" She squinted out over the town.

"I don't know," Remy said.

"So what did he say, your dad?"

Remy shrugged. "He wasn't exactly thrilled."

"Of course he isn't," Lisa said. "But it's not his life. It's yours. *Ours.*"

She laid her head on his shoulder and they sat until the sun went down and the mosquitoes drove them inside.

NINE

Remy walked in to work the next morning, ignoring the green glory of the mountain summer that surrounded him, wishing more than ever that he had a car. Walking was no good for someone with things on his mind he'd sort of like to forget. Like his dad's stony face over breakfast. He hadn't said more than the bare minimum to Remy since yesterday morning, and it was starting to get to Remy. Everything felt so turned upside down, it was hard to believe it wasn't even a week since he'd made the decision to go.

By the time he got to the garage, Duff was out front with a spray bottle and a roll of paper towels, scrubbing at the big office window. That was usually Remy's job.

"I'll do that," he told Duff.

"It's nearly done," Duff said.

Something was up. Remy sat down on an old tire and waited until Duff climbed down from the small ladder. "You missed a spot," he said.

"I heard you and Jimmy had a time for yourselves the other night."

"Oh. Yeah."

"Oh yeah," Duff echoed.

"So I guess Jimmy quit, huh?"

"No, Jimmy didn't quit. He didn't bother to quit." Duff threw the bottle of window cleaner through the office doorway and turned around in time to see Jimmy's car pulling into the station. "Jesus and the little fishes," Duff said under his breath and ducked into the office.

"Hey, Rem!" Jimmy climbed out of his car. "I been wondering what happened to you. When I saw Hanlon drag you out of Ferguson's, I thought for sure you were toast. What happened? He didn't haul you in, did he?"

"Nah, he took me home and—"

"There!" Duff came out of the office and threw a wad of bills at Jimmy. They hit Jimmy in the chest and scattered over the ground. Jimmy looked from the bills to Remy to Duff, open-mouthed.

"What the—?"

"That's what I owe you," Duff cut Jimmy off. "Take it and get out of here."

"What's your problem?"

"What's my problem?" Duff said. "You don't do your friends the way you did Remy and me, Jimmy. I don't care what you got going on, you don't walk off without a word to anyone about anything. And you sure as the devil don't take a seventeen-year-old kid into a bar and get him drunk and let the police carry him out!

Maybe you think you can do that and walk away, but you're gonna walk away knowing what I think of you."

Jimmy's face had gotten redder and redder as Duff talked, until his ears were nearly purple.

"Why should I care what you think?" he shouted. "You're just jealous because I'm getting out. You're a loser who didn't have the guts to get out himself, so you got to sit here and talk yourself into believing everyone else is wrong."

Jimmy pulled in a shaky breath and bent and scrabbled the money together.

"I'm sorry about Ferguson's," he said to Remy. "I was drunk and . . . I'm sorry. I—I'll see ya."

He got in his car and drove away.

Duff stood watching as the dust thrown up by Jimmy's car settled, then he turned around and kicked the cigarette sign over and sighed.

"You're not a loser, Duff," Remy said.

Duff laughed. "It looks like I'm short one mechanic. I've got a tricky valve job in here." He jerked his head toward the garage. "You want to come see what you can do with it?"

Remy spent the rest of the afternoon on the Lincoln's valves, glad to have the distraction. It was a big car, what Jimmy called a granny car, but with a powerful, impressive engine. When he started it up and leaned on the fender to check his work, the hum ran through the metal, into his palms and up his arms, like electricity. It gave him a sense that he knew this machine, that he'd had a part in keeping it running the way it was meant to run. It wasn't just another car or another engine. He knew the need, the desire for a car. But it was more than that, too, more than the utilitarian purpose of the machine. It was a sense of connection to a long line of minds that had designed and built and now kept running this metal animal, more powerful than two hundred horses. No wonder he felt electrified . . .

"That's sounding real good, Remy," Duff shouted over the engine.

Remy stepped back, breaking the connection, his palms still tingling from the contact. He watched while Duff poked around under the hood.

"Real good," Duff said again. He reached through the open window of the Lincoln and turned off the ignition. "You're good at this, y'know? You've got the hands for it."

"Coal-miner hands," Remy remembered Jimmy saying.

"No, it isn't about strength, not with an engine. It's about feel. You've got to be able to feel when it's right. It's a kind of sense. Doesn't mean a whole lot to some people, having a sense for a machine. But it sure means a lot when it's their machine that isn't working." Duff ran a cloth over the doorframe where he'd touched it. "Why don't you get the vacuum and do the interior, then do the windows, and we'll give Mr. Macklin a call and tell him his baby's ready."

Remy cleaned the Lincoln inside and out, rubbing it down with a chamois and a little bit of wax. Duff always liked sending a car back looking cleaner than when it came in. When Remy was done, it was past six and the air outside the garage hung heavy with the threat of a storm, thunder rumbling in the next valley over.

"You're welcome to stay here tonight," Duff said.

"Thanks, but I've got a new curfew now."

"You're lucky you're not looking at community service."

"I know."

"It's so easy to mess things up," Duff said to the sky. "Sometimes so bad there's no way of fixing it."

Remy turned to Duff. "You talking about me getting drunk?"

Duff shook his head. "I'm only talking. You'd better get on home. We're gonna have a gully washer."

Remy watched Duff walk into the garage, wondering what was eating him. To Remy, Duff had always seemed content, as satisfied as anyone he knew. He'd taken over the garage when his parents retired to Myrtle Beach, had their house up on the hill, wasn't hurting for friends. And girls, there was always a girl. Never anybody particular though, was there? Remy couldn't remember if Duff had ever had a serious girlfriend. But he mostly seemed happy. Except times like now . . .

But Remy had to get himself home. Walking. Seemed he spent an awful lot of his time walking. It wasn't easy walking either, up and down mountain roads. Wherever Lisa wanted him to go, probably nobody walked there. They all drove cars, nice cars, big SUVs like the tourists. His dad was right. He'd have to have a car if he was going to get a job. His thousand dollars wasn't enough for even a down payment on a new car. Couldn't afford the payments anyway, not with the kind of job he'd be able to get. If he'd gone to the technical school, he'd have his mechanic's certification now, could get a decent job. But would he still have Lisa?

Lightning flashed, showing him how dark it'd gotten, making the mountains stand out black around him. And the thunder, when it echoed down the bottom and ricocheted off the ridges, sounded like the mountains were cracking, breaking off and tumbling down into the valleys.

Did it feel like this, he wondered, where there were no mountains? You probably wouldn't miss the way rain smelled as it swept down over the ridge or the way it felt when the air trembled around you if you never knew it. But Remy knew. He stopped walking, stood with his eyes closed and let the thunder shake him.

"What are you doing? Are you crazy?!" someone was shouting.

Remy whipped around, saw the red Mustang.

"You want to get struck by lightning?" Dana shouted.

He grinned at her.

"Lightning's miles away."

But the minute he said it, there was a flash followed by another mountain-splitting crack of thunder. Dana squealed, and he couldn't help jumping a little himself.

"Help me put the top up and I'll give you a lift," she said.

"Are you sure? I thought I was a liability. Your insurance cover that?"

"Don't be stupid." Dana frowned, reaching for the release lever. "Anyway, I'm sorry about that. Can we blame it on the margaritas?"

Remy put up the top on the car, glad of the lift. For all his communing with the elements, he wasn't dumb enough to love the idea of hiking up the hollow in the pouring rain. He climbed in beside Dana as the first fat drops pelted the windshield.

"Do you have a death wish or something?" she asked him as she pulled back out into the road.

"Nah." He felt foolish now. Dana wouldn't understand what he'd felt. "I do it all the time. How do you think I got this electric personality?"

She groaned. "I can't believe you said that! You've got to tell me

97

which way to go," she said, peering through the rain. "I have trouble here even when I can see."

So he told her which roads to take.

Every time the thunder boomed, she jumped. "Is it always like this? When it storms, I mean? This is really bad. Isn't it?"

"This is a pretty good one," he said. "But it's not unusual. God isn't punishing us, if that's what you mean."

"It seems pretty bad to me." She was leaning so far forward that she was almost lying on the steering wheel. The rain sheeted her windshield between swipes of the wiper blades.

"You're not used to the way the thunder sounds when it bounces off the mountains," he told her. "The tourists always freak out when it storms here, afraid they're gonna get washed away."

"But that doesn't happen, right?"

"Not from a regular old thunderstorm. Back in May though, we had four days of heavy rain and it all came down the valleys and washed away dozens of houses and cars." Remy looked out the window. "It was bad. Lots of people lost everything and had to leave."

"Why did they have to leave? Couldn't they just rebuild?" Dana had relaxed a little, leaning back in her seat.

"Most of them didn't have insurance or the houses weren't theirs to begin with," Remy said. "And they couldn't afford to build something new, not here where it won't be worth anything. It's what the banks call a bad investment."

"So they just left?"

Remy shrugged. "They had to, whether they wanted to or not."

"The dark side of the challenge," she said.

"Huh?" And then he remembered what she'd said up at the high school, about the mountains. "Oh, yeah."

"But in a way, it's kind of . . . heroic, don't you think?" Dana glanced at him. "The people who stay have to be strong."

"Or crazy," Remy said. "You know over in Cincinnati, there's a whole ex-hillbilly colony? They even have something they call the Urban Appalachian Council, so the mountain people can keep in touch with their cultural roots. Isn't that funny? Like we're an endangered species or something. Turn right at the next road."

"Endangered species?" Dana's eyes slid over him. "Sounds like someone ought to slap you in a cage, make you part of some kind of captive breeding program."

"In your dreams."

He could almost feel her eyes on him, like when she'd run her fingertips along his skin. They were those kind of eyes. And he couldn't deny what that did to him. He was curious, couldn't deny that, either. But it was like being curious how it felt to be struck by lightning. You might wonder, but you didn't climb up on the roof during a storm to find out.

"You can drop me off here," he said, taking himself out of the game at the end of Walker Hollow Road.

"Where do you live?" Dana hesitated, squinting through the streaming rain.

"Up the hollow. It's not far, don't worry. Just stop here."

"It's pouring," she protested.

"No, honestly, just drop me here." He felt a stir of panic. What would she think of how he lived? "Please stop."

She only waved her hand at him. "Walker Hollow Road?" she

asked as they passed the sign at the corner. "As in Remy Walker?"

"It's not named after me personally," he said. "But it's the same family."

"Cool. You've got your own road and everything."

"Only because we've been here forever, back when this was still part of Virginia. So it's always been Walker Hollow because it was Walkers settled here."

"That's amazing," she said. "I mean, knowing that your family has lived here so long, to have that kind of connection to a place."

What did it look like to her as she drove? Didn't she see that the settlement at the mouth of the hollow was no more than a few old tin-roof houses, looking worse in the rain, like they were made of cardboard and could crumble at any second? He couldn't tell what Dana was thinking.

"You own this?" she asked.

"Not the hollow," he said. "My dad owns most of the mountain."

"Wow! Really? Is it Walker Mountain?"

She sounded impressed, not disgusted. But then she didn't know about the mountain.

"Yeah. It doesn't mean what you think it means, though. It isn't worth anything, the mountain. Not in money."

Even as he said it, he felt like he was betraying someone or something. It was what other people said about the mountain, never what he had felt.

"Yeah, but still. You *own* a mountain. That is very cool."

He watched her face, trying to figure out if she was playing around, making fun of him, but if she was, she was good at hiding it.

"Why isn't it worth anything? Land is always valuable," she said, like a girl from the suburbs where half an acre was an estate.

"It's only worth what someone else thinks it's worth," Remy said. "Nobody wants to live here. No coal underneath. At least, none worth going after."

"Is that all that matters?"

"What would you use it for?"

"I don't know. I'd just love it."

Remy couldn't look at her anymore and turned to watch the rain coming down on the mountain he had always loved. She could say she loved it without knowing what it meant, like singing a sad song when you'd never really felt the lyrics.

"That's a luxury," he said to the window.

"What?"

"I live up there," he said, pointing to the stone drive to the trailer.

Dana stopped the car and stared at his trailer. In the wet dark, the lights shone out like home, and Remy wondered again what it looked like to Dana. Did she see a home or a tin can dropped on the mountainside? She could love a mountain, but she couldn't love the way you had to live on it. Not that he blamed her. Not many people could. Not his mother. Not Lisa. If they heard the challenge of the mountains, it didn't mean anything to them.

"Thanks for the ride." He got out and slammed the door before she could say anything, and, hunching against the rain, he ran into the trailer.

T E N

"Remy, do you mind explaining to me what you think you're do-ing?" Remy's dad kicked the sole of Remy's boot, the only thing that was sticking out from under the bottom of their trailer.

"I'm fixing the plumbing!" Remy shouted, and heard his dad swear not quite under his breath. Well, so what? He hadn't been able to sleep, so he'd come out at dawn in the new-washed air, the leaves still dripping rain, and sat in the dappled shade of "his" mountain and thought.

There were all kinds of ways of living, that was clear. Some-times you didn't have a lot of choices. Then there was such a thing as letting living slide into something closer to existing. He started to get a scary feeling—a tickle in his gut—that that's where he and his dad had been heading.

So he'd gathered up the tools to tackle the thing most folks would consider stood between them and the basic definition of civilization: indoor plumbing.

"You know there's probably snakes under there," his dad said.

"There were," Remy said, surprised at how hard it was to make his voice sound normal while his dad could talk like there was nothing going on between them. "A couple of blacksnakes."

The first one he'd seen right away. But the second one had been curled up in the underbelly of the trailer, and when his banging chased it out Remy wasn't sure he wanted to admit which one of them was more scared. He was supposed to be a snake-wrangling mountain man.

"All right then." His dad sighed. "As long as you're happy . . . I gotta go into town. I won't be back till after lunch."

"What are you going to town for?"

If it was for a job, his dad usually told him so. His dad only shouted back, "See you later!" By the time Remy had wriggled out from under the trailer, the truck was rumbling away down the road. To see the Perkinses, Remy figured, ask them what they thought about Remy and Lisa's plans.

So Remy went back to work. He wasn't exactly sure what he was doing, though he figured he knew the basic principles, but after three frustrating hours, he still couldn't get water to come up into the toilet or the shower.

He was sitting on the big rock at the bottom of his dad's garden, mud down his backside, drinking a Pepsi, when a car crunched up the drive. He didn't recognize whose it was right away, though he knew the make, a '74 Chevy Nova, all gray primer and patches of body putty, the engine running rough and burning oil. The driver pulled up, and the engine coughed a couple of times before it cut off. Remy stood up.

Jimmy climbed out of the car and tossed the keys to Remy.

"A going-away present," Jimmy said.

"What the—?" Remy started walking a wide circle around the car. "This is your old Nova?"

"It's your old Nova, now." Jimmy leaned against the front end. "Or it will be after we go visit a notary."

"I didn't know you still had this."

It was four years ago Jimmy bought the Nova with money his grandmother left him. Remy'd thought it was the coolest thing he'd ever seen, even if it was the color of a rotten orange and the engine was all for crap. Jimmy was full of plans, was going to paint it candy-apple red, put in leather seats, rebuild the engine, new chrome . . . Remy could see that dream car as perfectly in his own mind as if the dream was his and was near eaten up with envy. But the Nova got put up on blocks and Jimmy bought a three-year-old Taurus and Remy forgot about the Nova.

"I been working on it a little. The bodywork's pretty much done." Jimmy ran a hand over the fender. "Maybe it could use a little sanding."

Walking sideways, Remy made it around the Nova without taking his eyes off it once, following the lines of the body. Now he stood next to Jimmy, shaking his head.

"You can't give this to me."

"Sure I can. You'll have to pay tax on it when we transfer the title, but it won't be much."

Remy shook his head. "Jimmy, this car is worth some money. More than I can afford. You can't just give it to me."

"Yeah, I can," Jimmy said. "Look, it isn't worth that much. It needs a paint job and the engine needs some work. But it's got four good tires and hey, the radio works."

Remy stared at the dull gray car and fingered the keys in his hand. He wanted it more than almost anything he'd ever seen.

"Naw, Jimmy. I can't take it."

"Remy," Jimmy said, "you're the best friend I ever had. And I can't believe you're making me say this, but I want you to have this car. I gotta get rid of it 'cause I know Kayla isn't going to let me bring it to Virginia."

"But you could sell it."

"I'm telling you, it isn't worth the hassle."

Remy chewed on his bottom lip. "What's Kayla think about giving it away?"

"She don't even know this car exists." Jimmy laughed. "I been keeping it up in the barn behind my brother's house. I was never going to finish it anyway. You know that. That engine's beyond me, but you could fix it. Duff'll help you. You ought to have it. It belongs to you."

"Ahhh, Jimmy . . ."

Jimmy threw an arm across Remy's back and gave him a couple of quick whacks to the shoulder blade.

"Come on, let's go make it legal."

Remy dropped Jimmy off and drove the car home. His car. He knew people who named their cars and thought it was the dumbest thing he ever heard of, but now he found himself thinking of names. Kirsten, for a girl he'd had a crush on in middle school, but had been too shy to do anything about and then she moved and it was too late. Or no, maybe Cassie, the prettier of the two models on the Harvey Tool calendar. Cassie was the perfect name.

He had a car! He revved the engine—just a little—at the one traffic light in town. It sounded like crap, and the whole thing was surrounded in a faint blue haze of burning oil, but it was his crappy, oil-burning engine. And it was all fixable. Car like this, it was pure mechanics. No touchy computers and electronic circuitry to fuss with. He couldn't wait to get under the hood and see what he could do.

He wanted to show someone, wanted to cruise through town. Lisa! He pictured Lisa sitting next to him on the bench seat, his arm around her shoulder, as he drove his cool car through the mountain roads he knew so well, windows open, the mountain air playing around them as miles and miles of green flashed by. He had to show Lisa, so he swung a left onto Bluebird Street and pulled up in front of the Perkinses' house, blowing the horn.

Scott came running out first and fell on his back, laughing.

"Where'd you get that old piece of junk?"

"Junk?" Remy climbed out of the car. "This is a classic."

"A classic piece of junk!"

Remy pinned Scott down with his knee and pulled a few WWF moves on him.

"Listen, stubby. In four years, you're going to be begging me to let you stand next to it."

"In four years, you aren't even going to be here." Scott wriggled out of Remy's grasp. "You're going off with my sister. I heard her arguing with Mom and Dad last night. They said she ought to—"

"Scott," Lisa said, coming down the cement steps. "Momma told you to clean Rascal's cage."

"Look what Remy got!" Scott scrambled to his feet and pointed.

Lisa looked at the car like it was some old stray dog. "Go on, Scott. Get. Or I'll tell Momma what really happened to the good teaspoons."

Remy got to his feet and braced himself. Lisa watched until Scott disappeared into the house. Then she turned around, arms crossed tightly across her waist, and jerked her head at Cassie.

"Where'd you get *that*?"

"Jimmy gave it to me." Remy felt like a three-day-old helium balloon, coming slowly back down to the ground, wind-in-the-hair driving fantasies evaporated.

"How much did you have to pay for it?"

"Nothing. He gave it to me. Well, I had to pay tax, but that's it." Lisa didn't say anything, just kept staring. "I know it doesn't look like much now. It needs some work, but once I get the engine running good and get it painted, it'll be sweet." He was running out of things to say and Lisa was still staring. "It's a classic," he added lamely.

"What are you going to do with it?" Lisa asked.

He looked at her like he wasn't sure he'd heard her right. Then he looked at Cassie, seeing her the way Lisa must.

"I'm going to drive it."

"You're not taking it along?" Now she was the one who sounded like she hadn't heard right. It was as if they were suddenly standing on separate planets, shouting incoherently at each other.

"Well, yeah . . ." Of course he was going to take it along!

"Will it even make it to Pennsylvania?"

"Sure it will, when I get it fixed up." He had to check himself, make sure he didn't call the car "her" in front of Lisa. "Duff'll help me."

She just needed to use her imagination a little, try to see the possibilities.

"And how much will that cost, fixing it up?" She stared at him.

"I don't know." His balloon was completely flat. "I haven't had a chance to really look at the engine yet. It needs a pretty good overhaul. And probably new tires. It doesn't need to be painted right away . . ."

"I think you ought to sell it," Lisa said.

"What?"

There she went again, talking some other language. In the whole two hours he had owned it, it had never for a split second entered his head that he might sell the car.

"You said it's a classic. It ought to be worth some money."

"Fixed up, maybe, but not like this." He looked at Cassie, stretched out along the curb like a fat gray cat, and saw her all shiny and red, with new rims and maybe a black pinstripe down the side. "I don't want to sell it. Besides, I'm going to need a car to get to work."

"Momma's going to give me her car," Lisa said. "Then we'll have to find a place that's either close to the college or close to your work and one of us will have to walk or take a bus or something. It'll have to do."

"Why does it have to do?" Remy asked. "Why can't we each have a car? I thought you had the money thing worked out."

"Well, things have changed." Lisa slumped down onto the steps. "Momma and Daddy aren't going to pay for an apartment. They want me to live in the dorms. They don't want me to live with you. They think I need some time away from you, that we're too 'heavy.' God, what a stupid word!"

Remy crouched next to her, remembering his dad going off that morning and not saying where.

"My dad didn't come and talk to them today, did he?"

"No. They thought this up on their own." She sighed.

"It'll be all right, honey. It doesn't matter what they think, right?"

Lisa's shoulders started to shake, so he sat next to her and held her while she cried.

"I'm sorry—I'm sorry about the car." Her voice cracked and she gulped hard. "But I was so mad. They want to make everything hard for us. It's not fair."

"It's okay," he said again, feeling it himself this time, glad to know that it was only her being mad at her parents. If it wasn't for that, he was sure she'd have joined him in his excitement about the car.

"They said to wait a year and maybe they'd pay for an apartment next year," she sobbed against him. "Because they think we'll change our minds. Like we'd forget about each other in a year!"

Remy didn't know what to say, still dazed by knowing Lisa's parents wanted him out of her life. He wasn't good enough. That's what it came down to. Saying "wait a year" was saying you'll find out he isn't important. Never in his life had he ever thought of himself that way, as not being good enough for any sort of thing. He'd always fit into life. And now it felt like someone put a hand flat on his chest and pushed him back. He wanted to jump up and take the cement steps three at a time and kick in the Perkinses' stained-glass door.

Only fifteen minutes ago, he was near about as happy as he'd ever been.

"What did you tell them?"

Lisa shrugged. "I told them I didn't care what they thought and that they were wrong." She turned in his arms so she could look at him, her eyes and the end of her nose red from crying. "We have to figure out a way to make it work, then we can show them how wrong they are. Do you see? You have to sell that car. We have to be really, really careful about money."

Remy looked past her to the car. It had only been his for a couple of hours, and before that, he'd had no idea it was even coming his way. Still, he didn't want to sell it, but if it meant that it could make it possible to be with Lisa . . .

"Hey, I just thought of something." He was stunned by the sheer brilliance of his idea. "Why can't we sell your momma's car? I mean, once we get to Pennsylvania, so she doesn't have to know right away. It'd be worth a heck of a lot more than this car."

"Are you serious?" Lisa's eyebrows scrunched together.

"Why not?"

She pulled away from him.

"Because Momma's car is only four years old, Remy. Not four hundred like that old thing." She waved her hand toward the Nova without looking at it. "We need a reliable car."

"I can make it reliable," he said, working hard to keep his voice quiet and steady. "And I'll be working in a garage, so if it does need work, I can get it done cheap, probably."

"How do you know where you'll be working?"

There it was again, that sense that they were missing each other by a mile. What was she talking about?

"I don't know *where* exactly," he said. "I'll find a job in some garage."

"Are you sure it'll be in a garage? You might have to get a job doing something else."

"But I don't have experience doing anything else. Just working on cars." He couldn't picture himself doing anything else. "It's what I want to do."

"But we can't think like that now, doing something because it's what you want to do. We don't have that luxury. We're going to have to make some sacrifices to make this work."

It seemed to him that the sacrifices were all his. He didn't say so, but she must have seen it in his face.

"This is going to be hard for me, too," she said. "I don't want to have to worry about money while I'm trying to study and go to class. But it's worth it to be with you, instead of doing what my parents want."

"I don't know."

Remy stood, his hands jammed into his back pockets, and looked out over Dwyer. Everything was going wrong. It wasn't supposed to be about sacrifices, but about doing what they wanted, both of them.

"I don't know." He couldn't trust himself to say any more.

"Oh!" Lisa got to her feet. "What does it matter what you do? It's not like working in a garage is a career or something!"

It was another sucker punch, only he knew she wasn't deliberately taking a jab at him. It was how she saw things. He stared at her, feeling like he'd swallowed his own heart, and wondered why she still looked the same when it felt like he was seeing her in a whole new way.

"I gotta go." He couldn't talk to her just now. That much he knew. He'd say something he could never make right. So he turned and started down the steps.

"Are you serious?" she shouted after him. "Now *you're* mad at *me*?"

He didn't turn around. Couldn't. He was mad, but it wasn't limited to her. He had a heck of a list all of a sudden.

"Fine. Go!" Lisa shouted after him.

He climbed into his car and pulled away.

ELEVEN

They'd never had a fight before, him and Lisa. Not in the two and a half years they'd been together. Sure, Lisa'd get mad at him every now and then, but it never lasted long. So he didn't know, wasn't sure what this fight meant. With nothing to measure it against, how could he tell how bad it was? It felt like someone had cut him open.

Out of all the reasons he had to be angry, the thing that rankled the most was how quickly his pleasure over the car had been squashed. He never should have stopped at Lisa's. He should have taken the car and kept on driving. Taken some time to enjoy what he had. Now he'd always associate this fight with the car.

His dad still wasn't back when he pulled up next to the trailer. Remy went inside and came back out with the tools, propped up Cassie's hood, and started poking around the engine. Didn't look like Jimmy'd done anything with it the whole time he had it. It needed a tune-up bad. The spark plugs were vintage, and the belts should probably be changed. It was typical Jimmy to worry about making the outside look good first. He wondered how hard it was going to be to get the parts he'd need. He was so intent on the engine, he didn't hear his dad pull up in the truck.

"Where'd this come from?" his dad asked. This time, he couldn't make it sound like nothing was wrong between them. It stood out a mile, filled in the distance between them with uncomfortable questions.

"Jimmy sold it to me." Remy lowered the hood. "I mean, he gave it to me," he said before his dad could explode over him spending his money on an old piece-of-junk car. "But I had to pay tax on it. Sixty-two fifty."

"Sixty-two fifty?" His dad walked around the car. "Well, it might be worth a little more than that."

"Yeah." Remy couldn't laugh. He was too sore. Sore about Cassie, about the Perkinses, everything.

"I guess we got some things to talk about," his dad said.

Remy didn't respond, just wiped his hands on an old towel. He noticed his dad was wearing a striped shirt so crisp it looked like brand-new, gray trousers, and shoes all shined up.

"I don't want to tell you what to do with your life," his dad said. "But I do want to ask you to really think before you make a real big decision like this."

"You think I haven't?"

"No, but it won't hurt to do it some more."

"What's there to think about?" As if the afternoon hadn't dumped a ton of things to consider in his lap. "We're not stupid. We've thought about everything like rent and bills and stuff. I know as much about that as you do."

"I don't mean details. I'm talking about why. Why are you doing this? You say you love Lisa and you want to be with her. Now"—his dad held up a hand to stop Remy interrupting him—"I'm not saying that isn't a good enough reason."

"Then what's the big deal?" Remy said it louder, more exasperated than he meant.

"Remy, I don't want to fight with you, but sometimes it's hard to see things the way they really are when you are bound and determined to see them some other way. You know what I mean?"

"No, I don't," Remy said.

"Then let me ask you a question. You want to tell me who that little girl was that brought you home in the Mustang last night?"

"Dana?" Remy said without thinking.

"Don't know any Dana." His dad made a show of peering into the trees and scratching his chin.

"She's from up around Martinsburg." Remy tried to cover the damage. "She's down here painting the water tower, came to the garage a couple of times."

"That all?"

"Yeah, that's all." Remy looked hard at his dad, trying to figure out where he was going with this.

"I hope you're sure," his dad said. "I hope every girl who comes along is just another girl and that Lisa is the only one you're ever going to want your whole life. Because that's what you're saying. You're going to up and change everything because you are that certain. So you tell me right now. Tell me that that girl Dana is only someone who gave you a lift and Lisa is the girl you're going to love forever and then I'll believe you when you say you know what you're doing, leaving here."

Remy didn't have words to describe what Dana was because he

didn't know. But Lisa . . . he loved Lisa. Even now, still aching and unsure from the afternoon, there was that sense of quiet comfort inside from thinking about her, the way she made him feel bigger and more important than the mountains because he belonged to her.

"If you want to leave because you think you want a better life somewhere else," his dad went on, "then fine. I can deal with that. I'll even stand behind you. But if there's something else going on, then you got to let me know. Which is it?"

The words tumbled out in a kind of rambling urgency Remy'd never heard before, his dad's usual quiet drawl ramped up to top speed.

"I already told you," Remy said. "But why is it so important right now?"

His dad ran a hand along the side of the Nova.

"I need to know because I got an offer on this land," he said without looking at Remy.

"What?"

"Yeah, about a month ago, letter came from Mountaineer State Mining Company."

"Dad!" Remy choked on shock. "They're the ones doing the mountaintop removal mining around here. That's what caused that bad flooding. You can't sell Walker Mountain to them!"

"Hold on a second. They're not going to mountain-top Walker Mountain. There ain't enough coal here to even make that kind of mining worthwhile. They need it for access to Jenner and Little Bar mountains. Of course that means they ain't paying much, but it'd be enough."

"For what?" Remy never would have believed he'd hear his dad talking seriously about any such thing. His mind scrambled to make sense of it.

"It'd make it so I could give you enough money to make a good start in Pennsylvania."

"I don't— Dad—" His brain was spinning. "You can't do it, Dad. I don't need anything."

His dad shook his head. "You can't go to Pennsylvania with one thousand dollars and a beat-up old car. It ain't just living money. This'd be enough so that you could take a mechanic's certification course. I went to the library and looked on the Internet. Look here." He came around to the front of the car, pulling a wad of papers from his pocket. "I printed some stuff for you." He unfolded them and spread them out on the hood. "Here's one right in the same town where you'd be living, only takes nine months, and then you'd be able to get a real good job."

Remy couldn't look at them. He mumbled, "Dad, you can't sell Walker Mountain. Not to the mining company. You just can't."

Gone. He couldn't conceive of this place—this place that had always felt like a part of him—belonging to someone else. Not even belonging, being used in the worst way: to get to other mountains and tear them down.

"God knows, Remy, I don't have much to give you, but I can give you this. This here . . ." His dad paused and Remy could sense him taking in the trailer, the mountain. "This is a hard way to live. It ain't for everyone. I should've thought of that long ago, that this was no place for you to build a future on. But I don't want you to have to go out and work in some carpet factory. If you're leaving here to have a better life, then you'd better be doing something that makes you happy."

His dad understood what Lisa didn't. But how was Remy supposed to know what would make him happy when it was tangled like this?

"Is that where you went today? All dressed up?" he asked his dad.

"I went down to their office in Bluefield."

"Is it settled? I mean, did you sign something?"

"No, it was just a meeting. They're making offers, but nothing definite yet," his dad said. "I wasn't even going to consider it, but after what you told me yesterday, I started thinking it was the best thing to do." He concentrated on refolding the library papers. "So you see, that's why I need to know. Pretty soon."

"What about you?" Remy asked.

"Don't worry about me," his dad said. "There'll be plenty left for me, too. I'll get a place in town."

There'd been Walkers living on this mountain for more than a hundred and sixty years, before there ever was a town. They were hard, tough people, those Walkers. It took people like that to live in a place like this. The mountains suited them, the shape of the mountain, the fall of its shadow, the scent of its earth, was part of their bloodline. Now it was down to him, whether there'd still be Walkers or not on Walker Mountain. He couldn't make a decision like that so fast.

"I want to say something," he told his dad, "but I don't want you jumping on me right away and saying it means anything. Let me get it out."

"Okay."

"I need some time to think about this." He rushed to add, "Now don't tell me if I was sure, I wouldn't have to think about it.

There's a lot more to it now than how I feel about Lisa. You really threw a wild card into it, Dad. You know that."

"I know," his dad said. "But we've got to make a decision on this soon, so we can get it settled and get the money in time."

Remy frowned. "How soon?"

"I don't know. Next week, probably?"

A week to decide whether or not to irreversibly turn the world upside down, to turn his dad out of his home, to break the connection of a hundred and sixty years. Remy bent and started gathering up the tools.

"I have to talk to Lisa." Except Lisa probably wasn't talking to him.

"Here."

His dad held out the library papers. Remy slipped them in his back pocket and walked around to get in the car. His dad stopped halfway to the trailer.

"Oh! How'd the plumbing go?"

"Not so good," Remy said. "I thought I had it fixed, but I couldn't get the water to come up in the pipes."

"I'll take a look," his dad said. "Sometimes air gets in there and you need to bleed it out. It'd be nice to have a shower here again."

Remy climbed into Cassie—not even thinking that selling the mountain would mean he could keep Cassie. That wasn't as important as it had been an hour ago. He started his car and drove back to town.

TWELVE

Lisa wasn't home. Her mother told him, as sweet as could be, like she thought he didn't know what she really felt about him.

"Hello, Remy! Why no, Lisa isn't here. Went off with a couple of her girlfriends. No, I don't know where, I'm sorry."

He felt like tossing it back at her, letting her know what he knew. Felt like saying, "Thanks anyway, Mrs. Perkins. I guess I'd better get used to the idea of not seeing Lisa much and get back to being unworthy, maybe go find me some welfare girl to hook up with and sign up for food stamps." Instead, he thanked her and climbed in his car.

A couple of her girlfriends. That meant Bree and Tracy. He needed to talk to Lisa bad, but not bad enough to track her down at one of her friends' houses. His dad's news paced in his mind like a caged wildcat. But it would have to stay there for now. Besides, he was hungry. He hadn't eaten anything all day except a handful of Oreo cookies at the notary. So he headed for Loretta's Diner, thinking he'd grab something to eat and maybe swing by

Duff's, have him take a look at Cassie. Maybe Lisa'd be back home after that.

When he pulled into the parking lot at Loretta's, his eyes were automatically drawn to Dana's red Mustang. She saw him, too. Or she saw Cassie, turning in her seat to look, smiling when she recognized him, and letting out a whistle. Remy parked next to her.

"Don't tell me you're a biscuit convert!" he shouted at her.

"Loretta does a mean Caesar salad." She came over to look at Cassie. "Where'd you get this?!"

He told her, watching the appreciative way her eyes followed the line of the Nova.

"This is one amazing car." She leaned back, her hands on the door. "Seventy-three?"

"Seventy-four." He couldn't quite keep the surprise out of his voice. He didn't know any girls who knew about cars.

"It needs a lot of work," he said apologetically.

"Oh yeah, but it'll be great." She stuck her head in the window and he ducked back in time to avoid getting head-butted. "Original interior?"

"Yeah. It's not too bad." He ran a hand over the upholstery.

She smiled at him. "Don't look so surprised. My dad has a '69 Camaro he restored himself. I grew up at classic car shows."

It was impossible to listen to her and not think about how different Lisa's reaction had been.

"Aren't you going to take me for a ride?" Dana asked.

"I don't think she's up for a real run, yet." The thought of Dana sitting next to him cut a little too far into his fantasy of driving out with Lisa. "In fact, I'm taking her over to Duff's now, have him take a look at her."

"Her, huh?" Dana raised an eyebrow at him and he felt his face go hot. It'd slipped out, the "her" thing. "I bet she has a name and everything," Dana said.

Remy couldn't help laughing.

"Let me guess." She rolled her eyes. "It starts with 'L.' "

"Actually," he said, "she's named after the girl in the Harvey Tool calendar."

"Oh my God. Not the chesty one!"

"Yeah, Cassie!"

"That's actually reassuring." She straightened up. "It's good to know you have some typical flaws. I was starting to think you were almost perfect."

She headed back to her car, and he called after her.

"What's wrong with being perfect?"

She looked over her shoulder. "Nothing."

She got in her car and drove off, leaving Remy to watch her go and wonder what the heck she meant.

"It's nice, Remy." Duff wiped his hands on a cloth, still admiring Cassie's engine. "I don't know, maybe being encrusted with two inches of crud protected it or something. Or maybe the angels were watching out for it. But considering how long Jimmy owned it, it looks darned good."

"So you don't think it needs to be rebuilt?" Remy asked.

"Nah. It needs a good tune-up and the belts need replacing pretty bad. I wouldn't drive it too far before you did that much. And it's burning a little oil, but I think we can fix that easy enough. Bring it in when you come to work tomorrow and if we get some downtime, we'll get started on it."

"Thanks, Duff."

He would've hugged Duff if Matt hadn't been standing there. Duff's evaluation of Cassie's prognosis restored some of that flying happiness he'd felt when Jimmy signed the car over.

"That was a nice thing Jimmy did," Duff said. "You could really have yourself something here."

He could. Driving back over to Lisa's, the sky darkening from purple to navy blue, he thought about what it could mean, his dad's offer. To have the money to go, be with Lisa, go to school and get his mechanic's certification, and even keep this car. Everything he wanted was right there. Then why did it feel like such a life or death choice? The gates wouldn't be locked behind him if he left. Even if the mountain was sold, Dwyer would still be here, surrounded by plenty of other mountains. It wasn't going to disappear like a village in a fairy tale the minute he stepped away. Plenty of people moved all the time, sometimes across oceans. Heck, it was always a big deal at the family reunion, talking about Andrew and Dovie Walker, coming the whole way from Scotland to McGuire County in 1840. Seemed like it was a family tradition, to get up and go, looking for something better.

He pulled over in front of the Perkinses' house. If he didn't get to talk to Lisa soon, he'd go crazy. But Lisa wouldn't come to the door.

"I need to talk to her," he told Mrs. Perkins. "Just for a minute. Please tell her it's important."

"I'm sorry, Remy," Mrs. Perkins said. "I'm not going to get in the middle of this." She started to close the door and stopped to say, "Lisa was very upset when she came home tonight." And closed the door in his face—but gently.

Lisa was mad, he knew that. She went and told her friends and they got her stirred up and now she was upset and wouldn't even talk to him. She had to know, he had to tell her how everything could work out.

On the sidewalk, he stood and looked up at her window. She was in there watching TV and he was out here with a raging wildcat in his head and there was nothing he could do about it.

THIRTEEN

Hey, come on in here." Remy's dad shook him awake. "I want to show you something."

What now? Remy'd about had his fill of surprises and shocks. But he got up and trailed him into the bathroom, where his dad reached into the shower and twisted the knob.

"Ta da!" he said, like a magician.

With a sputter, a strong spray of water shot out of the shower-head.

"You did it," Remy said. "You fixed it."

"Nah. You fixed it. I finished it up for you. Go on. You get the honor of the first shower. Handyman's rights."

"If you're trying to tell me I stink," Remy said, "you could just say so."

"You ain't exactly curling the hairs in my nose, but you could use a scrub." His dad tossed him a towel and backed out of the bathroom.

Amazing, Remy thought, hot water pounding on his head, how luxurious something so basic could feel. How the things that people took for granted, wouldn't have counted among the pleasures of their lives, could make you so happy if you let them. A hot shower close at hand and the smell of ham frying in the kitchen was enough. Having just enough ought to *be* enough to make anyone happy. He pulled on his jeans and padded into the kitchen, rubbing his hair dry with a towel.

"Wow, you made biscuits." Remy swung his leg over a kitchen chair and sat down to a plate of ham, biscuits, and gravy.

"Just the Bisquick kind," his dad said. "I never could get the hang of making them from scratch. Your grandma could do it in her sleep."

"They're good," Remy said around a mouthful.

"That reminds me, Aunt Vennie's been pestering about the reunion."

"Why does that remind you of Aunt Vennie?"

"I don't know." His dad sat down and lit a cigarette, blew the smoke at the ceiling. "The reunion's on the eleventh. You're coming, right? You got off work?"

"Yeah—oh . . ." Remy swore. "I forgot about Jimmy quitting. Duff's shorthanded now. I don't know if he'll get someone in by then."

"He'll have to deal with Vennie if you don't show up at that reunion." His dad took a long drag, exhaled again. "Lisa coming?"

"I don't know." He hadn't got around to asking her, back when they were still talking.

"You get a chance to talk to her yet?"

That was a tough question. Remy swiped the rest of the gravy off his plate with a biscuit and crammed it in his mouth.

"Not yet," he mumbled. "She wasn't home last night. I'll try to hook up with her after work today."

"Okay, but I gotta know soon," his dad said. "They ain't going to sit on this forever."

"What happens if you don't agree?" Remy asked. "To sell, I mean. They can't force you to, can they?"

"Probably they could." His dad stubbed out his cigarette. "But it'd be a lot of trouble. There's other places they can get access, maybe over by Hager." He got up, stretched. "I'm going to go test out that shower myself."

Remy finished the last of the biscuits and washed up the dishes. The bare minimum of civilized living, he thought, and checked his watch. He wouldn't have time to see Lisa before work. The wildcat would have to be patient.

He was on foot again. Cassie was back at Duff's, her engine half tore apart, waiting for some parts Duff had ordered. In a way, he figured it was better like this, walking to Lisa's house, with no car to remind her of what sparked their disagreement. On the way through town, he thought it was funny how different everything seemed, like he'd grown up overnight or something. A week ago, it'd felt like being in a canyon, walking down Main Street. Now it seemed like an outgrown toy. It was as if his mind had made a leap and the rest of him needed to catch up. As he passed Lion's Park, a couple of guys he knew spotted him and shouted at him to come shoot hoops with them. But he only raised his hand at them and kept walking, feeling like it was a leave-taking almost. Every familiar shabby building he passed was one more quick goodbye. He was done. Done with Dwyer.

Passing the VFW, he had the urge to stick his head in the door, another leave-taking. Inside, his great-uncle Bernie and a couple of cronies in suspenders and soft hats were playing poker.

"Remy!" Joe Carroll called.

"Got any money? Then come on in and ante up!" Harry Davis laughed.

"Sorry, just passing by," Remy said.

"How's your dad, Rem?" Uncle Bernie asked.

"Hey," Joe said. "I heard they're trying to buy your daddy's land for mining. That true?"

"I told you," Harry said, "they'd have to run the dragline smack over Alvin before he'd sell Walker Mountain."

Remy only smiled. "I'll see you at the reunion, Uncle Bernie." Bernie nodded. Remy kept on down the street. Good old boys, they used to be miners or soldiers. Soldiers and miners. That's all there was for them back when they were his age. Nowadays, you had options, and his had just opened up.

Up ahead, he saw Lisa coming out of her dad's store and ran to catch up with her, grabbing her by the waist and swinging her around on the sidewalk, nearly knocking Mrs. Morse into the street.

"There's a time and place for that, Remy," Mrs. Morse said. "And Friday afternoon on the public street isn't it. I don't care what you see on TV." She huffed and went on her way.

"What is the matter with you?" Lisa wriggled out of his grasp, her face pulled with anger, and Remy remembered that they were fighting, that she didn't know.

"I gotta talk to you. Everything's fixed. It's all right."

"What's fixed?"

He told her about his dad's offer and watched her face slowly soften.

"Oh, Remy, he didn't!" But it was total disbelief and no sorrow. She sat down on the barrel of petunias on the street corner. "That's such a lot of money. We could—oh my God—Remy! I can't believe it. You're serious? You mean it's really going to happen, not just something they're talking about?"

"It's serious." He stood in front of her, dazzled by the look on her face. Lisa was worth anything. "That's why I had to find you and talk to you today. My dad needs to let them know right away and then they'll get the money settled."

For a second she sat, staring at nothing, and he could see her working it all out in her head, saw it play across her face, until she couldn't hold it in a second more. With a breathless "Oh!" she flew off the barrel and into his arms, whispering warm in his ear, "Take me away from here."

They walked down the railroad tracks along Rope River until they were out of sight of the town, of everything and everyone.

"I was so afraid," she said, holding his hand tight in both of hers.

"Of what?"

"That it was over. I don't know what I'd do without you."

"That's not something you'll ever have to find out," Remy said.

"We've never had a real fight." Her voice quivered with fear.

"This wasn't a real fight." He stopped and pulled her close, "We won't ever have one."

Sighing, Lisa laid her head on his chest. He stroked her hair and saw the letters on his arm—R.A.W.—and realized that it was gone, that raw feeling. That had to mean that he was doing the right thing.

FOURTEEN

For a week, Remy felt like he'd been caught up in a freshet, rushed along on top of the current, too exhilarated to worry about what was passing underneath.

Most of his time he divided between Lisa and work. Whenever there was a spare minute, he worked on Cassie with Duff. Remy only wanted to get her roadworthy, but Duff fussed at him, made him do the job right.

Lisa overflowed with excitement, making plans. Sometimes, she couldn't wait for him to get off work and would come chattering into the garage with stuff she'd printed out from the Internet about apartment complexes.

"Look, Remy, this one has a pool and a gym."

Remy wondered what had happened to the idea of a small apartment or even a room somewhere near the college, but she was so happy, he didn't think about it too much. Being around her now was like swimming in champagne, and he just wanted to enjoy the feeling, floating, surrounded by her bubbles, his head slightly reeling. It was good, and he didn't want anything flattening it.

The only thing that could were parents, his and hers. But his dad didn't say much, even when Remy told him he'd made up his mind about going. He only nodded, said, "Okay. As long as you're sure." And Remy tried not to remember what his face looked like when he said it. It'd be better for him, Remy told himself. He couldn't go on forever, digging out coal and scraping a living just to hang on to a worthless mountain. This way, it worked out for everyone.

When he called his mom to tell her, she was thrilled.

"Oh, honey, I'm so glad," she said. "It's a dead end there. It really is. And don't you worry about your daddy. Owning all them trees never did him any good anyway."

As for Lisa's parents . . .

"They'll come around when they see how serious we are," Lisa said. "They *do* like you, you know they do."

But Remy preferred to keep his distance. And he had a feeling her parents weren't going to give up that easy.

That next Friday, she was waiting for him after work, sitting on the wall by the old, empty SureSavr with Bree and Tracy. Remy stopped on the sidewalk and waved at her, hoping she'd just come so he wouldn't have to talk to her friends.

Lisa came, crossing the crumbling parking lot like she was crossing a ballroom. She slipped her hand in his and they walked so close, their hips touched, their steps automatically falling into a rhythm.

"I have to go away for a couple of weeks," she said to the sidewalk.

"What? Where are you going?" It was the first he'd heard of it.

"Momma wants me to go to South Carolina with Mrs. Hambro." She let out an impatient sigh. "She's going to visit her sister and Momma thinks she ought to have someone go with her. But I think Momma wants to get me away from you." She turned her face to him when she said "you," her eyes narrow, her mouth a tight line.

"Oh." Now he was talking to the sidewalk. He was willing to bet Mrs. Hambro had a say in it, too.

"I told her I knew what she was up to and I wasn't going to go." Lisa talked fast, spitting out the words. "But then Daddy joined in and they—well, there was a big fight and . . ." She shrugged. "They're making me go."

Remy didn't ask for details. They were in front of the courthouse, and he leaned against the base of one of the stone lions. Lisa wrapped her arms tight around his waist and butted her head up under his chin.

"It doesn't matter what they think," she said.

Maybe not, but it hurt.

"It's only for two weeks?" he said.

"Yeah. I don't know what they think is going to change in two weeks. And when I get back and your dad gives you the money, we'll go. Get out of here for good."

She pulled his head down and kissed him. A passing car blew the horn. Remy laughed and Lisa frowned.

"I hate this town!"

That Monday, she left early in the morning, earlier than had been planned, so they didn't even get to say goodbye. Remy went into work, complaining to Duff.

"You can't take it so personally," Duff said. "It isn't about you, Remy. It's about her and what they think she ought to be doing right now."

"How is it not about me when it's me they want to get her away from?" Remy banged the push broom through the garage.

"Because it's not you, specifically. They'd feel this way about any guy Lisa thought she was serious about just now."

"She *is* serious."

"Okay, okay." Duff held up his hands in surrender. "I'm just saying. And don't break my broom."

Everyone thought they were right because they'd "been there," been his age, made mistakes. But they didn't know because they had never been exactly like him and never had someone exactly like her. They didn't know.

Flat, that was the first week, the days moving slow. That was what it would be like without her, without Lisa. She filled his days, made everything have a reason beyond marking time. It was why he needed her and had to be with her.

Remy went to work, went home. Couldn't even get excited about the Fourth of July celebrations, with everyone else paired up on blankets behind the courthouse, watching the fireworks up on the ridge. On Wednesday, when he didn't have to work, he hung out with some school friends. They went mountain biking and tubed down Rope River, but Remy felt like he was on a kiddie ride at the carnival. His mind had moved on so fast and so far and was only waiting for his body to get on out of there and join it.

On Friday, Remy worked with Matt, but by the afternoon, traffic at the garage was dead.

"You might as well cut out," Matt said.

"Thanks, but I want to work on my car some," he told Matt.

"Gonna be a sweet ride." Matt trailed him over to Cassie. "Would you believe I had one of these new?"

"Yeah?"

"Had it almost fifteen years. My ex-wife plowed it into a tree. I still say she did it on purpose, figured it was worth a broke leg just to piss me off."

Pretty soon, they were both bent over Cassie's engine. When the bell rang for the pumps out front, Remy said, "I'll get it."

And there was Dana, smiling at him. "Hey, there."

Remy hadn't seen her in more than a week. She'd been in twice the week before, Duff told him, always asking where Remy was. Remy hadn't been deliberately avoiding her. It just worked out that he hadn't been there. But he was kind of glad, all the same. She . . . got inside his head. And she'd be gone soon anyway, he figured. It couldn't take much longer to paint that tower.

Now he walked around the back of the Mustang.

"Fill it up?"

"Actually . . ." She got out of the car and came over to where he was standing. She was wearing a red halter top, showing bare shoulders, brown and freckled, like her nose.

"Actually," she said again, looking at him, her eyes uncertain. "I need some help, and I didn't know anyone else to ask."

"What do you need?"

"Can you recommend a hotel nearby?"

"Why do you need a hotel?"

She looked dangerously like she might cry.

"Ian threw me out," she said.

"Why would he throw you out?" Remy asked. "What'd you do? Burn his stupid oven mitt collection?"

She laughed. "No, he—uh—" She hesitated, examined her shoes. Remy followed her gaze. She was wearing sturdy hikers, spattered with paint.

"That's okay, don't tell me," he said. "It's none of my business."

She caught his eyes, then, and for a minute studied his face.

"Yeah," she said. "Maybe that would be better."

"I don't know what to tell you about a hotel, though." He slid his hands into his coverall pockets. "There are two motels in town, but I'm betting they're probably both full up right now."

"I didn't realize this was such a tourist hot spot," Dana said.

"Not tourists. We're having a family reunion tomorrow, so if you need a room for more than tonight, you might be out of luck."

"That must be some family, if you can fill up two motels." She leaned her bottom against the back of her car.

"There's enough of us," Remy said. "But the motels aren't exactly huge."

"What am I going to do?" Dana kicked her car with her heel. "It's going to take me at least another week to finish up here!"

She did start crying then, head down, sniffling, arms hugging her chest. Remy didn't know where to look, torn between discomfort and wondering what had happened.

"If I have to pay for a hotel, it's going to eat up almost everything I'm getting paid!" Dana pressed her palms against her eyes.

Remy didn't know what to tell her. There was no way he could offer to let her stay at the trailer. There was a cot in the storage room of the garage, but she wouldn't want to stay there. There was one other possibility, and he didn't know why he was half-afraid to mention it. Maybe he was hoping she wouldn't be able to find a place to stay and would have to go, leave Rosella Banks half-painted on the water tower.

"My parents will love this. They'll think it's proof that everything they've been telling me about being an artist is right," Dana said, wiping her tears with the back of her hand.

"What did they say?" Remy thought painting water towers was a pretty useless way to spend your summer and the state's money, but he knew enough about wanting to do something that other people didn't think much of.

"Oh, you know." Dana sniffed and shrugged. "That you can't make a living as an artist, that I'm wasting my college money, that I ought to major in something practical and minor in art, that it can be my *hobby*." A short, hysterical laugh. "Remy, this isn't a hobby, it's my life. It's what I think about all the time. I can't imagine only being able to do it on weekends or something. But if I can't even make it work this summer, how can I make a living at it?"

She dropped her face in her hands and really cried, shoulders shaking. Loud enough to make Matt stick his head out of the garage, looking relieved when Remy waved him away. Remy knew he had to do something, part of him aching for her longing and her hurt, but he couldn't think of any other way to comfort her.

"Let's go talk to Arlette," he said finally.

"Who's Arlette?" Dana mumbled into her hands.

"She owns the Duke of Dee Motel. She might be able to work something out for you."

"But you said it was probably booked up."

"Arlette has a residence there," Remy said. "She's got an extra bedroom she sometimes lets out in special, emergency situations."

"I don't know if I can afford it." Dana straightened, ran her hands through her curls.

"We might be able to fix something," Remy said. "Arlette was my dad's high school sweetheart. She still has a thing for him, so . . . well, let's go talk to her."

He was relieved to see Dana smile a little.

"You are shameless," she said. "I hope your dad doesn't mind being dangled like a piece of meat."

"That there would be the difference between men and women," Remy said. He stuck his head in the garage and told Matt he was going to cut out after all and got in the Mustang with Dana, giving her directions to the Duke of Dee, partway up a ridge south of town, on this side of Walker Mountain.

Arlette didn't exactly snap at the bait, but Remy knew his approach definitely fell into the category of what his grandmother would have called wheedling.

"Too damned good-looking, like your daddy," Arlette said. "Just going to get yourself in trouble, if you aren't already. Come on up," she said to Dana, "and I'll show you the room. We'll let Remy bring your things in, see if he's good for more than sweet-talking old women."

"Miss Arlette, wait, you didn't say—" Dana called after her. "I mean, how much do you charge for the room?"

Arlette stopped at the bottom of the staircase. "Oh, honey, I don't charge people to stay in my house. And don't call me Miss Arlette. This isn't *Steel Magnolias.*"

"That's really nice of you—Arlette," Dana said. "But I have to pay you something."

"Don't you worry about it," Arlette said, winking at Remy. "I'll work it out with Remy's daddy later. Only my brother Everett is coming to visit third week of August and he doesn't like the motel rooms, so if you're not finished up by then, you'll have to move into the motel and I will have to charge you then, or my accountant will kill me. Alvin or no Alvin. Now come on. In case you haven't heard, we've got a busy weekend coming up and I've got a lot of work to do."

Remy carried Dana's things up to Arlette's spare room, glad not to have run into any Walker relatives, and Dana followed him back outside.

"Can I drive you back to the garage?" Dana asked. "Or home?"

"No, that's okay. I can walk."

She reached out a hand like she was going to touch him, then changed her mind and let it fall.

"Thank you so much, Remy. You saved my life."

"You can send me a plaque later."

He'd have done it for any friend, he told himself. Dana was a friend.

"Want to go get something to eat?" she asked.

You could go get something to eat with a friend. But maybe not when your girlfriend was out of town. And maybe not when that sad catch in your friend's voice did funny things to your stomach.

"Nah, thanks." Remy slid his hands into his pockets. "I've gotta get home."

He took a shortcut over the ridge to Walker Hollow, knowing the path by heart. It was a funny way of saying you remembered something as simple as a footpath, to say it was in your heart.

The whole way, he kept thinking about Dana and how his insides flipped at the thought of her crying, wanting to fix it for her, how good he felt when he did fix things. How hard it had been to walk away.

When he got home, his dad was in the garden, ripping out the spent sugar pea vines.

"I think I might have promised Arlette you'd take her out next weekend," Remy told him.

His dad didn't say anything, just pulled a paper out of his back pocket and handed it to Remy.

"What's this?"

"The terms Mountaineer State Coal is offering," his dad said flatly. "We had our meeting today. I signed a preliminary agreement. It'll be final in a month."

Remy slowly unfolded the paper and read, but the figures didn't seem to mean anything.

"I'd appreciate it if we could keep this between ourselves for a while, especially this weekend," his dad said. "I don't want to have to explain to the whole clan all at once."

"Okay," Remy said.

"I'm just sorry," his dad said to the sky. "I'm sorry it's come to this. I feel like there oughta been something I should have done somewhere along the line, but I don't know what."

"Dad—" Remy started, but his dad shook his head.

"Rather not talk about it just now, Remy." He tossed the vines onto a pile beside the garden and walked into the trailer.

Remy stood in the middle of the garden, the paper still in his hand, the paper that meant he got what he wanted. It would take getting used to, that's all. You could get used to anything.

But as Remy stepped across the neat furrows, he noticed something he hadn't seen before. His dad hadn't just ripped out the old pea vines. He'd ripped out everything. Every tomato plant, every cornstalk, pepper, onion, carrot. The potato hills and squash and melon mounds were flattened. All that was left was a heap of crushed stalks and wilted green leaves and barren, empty rows of dirt.

FIFTEEN

Now, I told you I don't want that canopy set up right there!"
Aunt Vennie shouted, hands on her hips. "People sitting in the
pavilion won't be able to see the amphitheater that way!" She bus-
tled between the picnic tables, muttering, "I swear, if anyone actually thought about what they were doing, I'd have a heart attack.
I'm the only one here with half a brain. Got to do the thinking for
everyone." She spotted Remy before he had a chance to escape and
grabbed his arm.

"Remy, honey, go on down there and tell those boys to move
that canopy about twenty feet to the right."

"Those boys" were his dad's cousins Gary, Don, and Frank,
and Uncle Bernie, none of them under forty. And Uncle Bernie was
past seventy. Remy started down the hill, Aunt Vennie calling after
him in a voice that probably carried over to the next valley.

"Then come on back up here and help me hang up these
speakers!"

"What does she need speakers for?" Frank said. "They can probably hear her in Kentucky."

They snorted and guffawed, and Remy helped them tear down the canopy and move it.

"Hey, what's this talk about Mountaineer State wanting to buy Walker Mountain?" Gary asked.

"That's just a rumor," Uncle Bernie said. "They're always talking, right, Remy?"

"Yeah, I guess." Remy concentrated on tying one of the canopy ropes to a stake. "I haven't heard anything."

It was a lie and they were going to be mad when they found out. And that wasn't all. They didn't have any legal claim to the mountain, but they were only a generation or so removed from it. Not to mention the whole idea of mountain topping. Even though most of the family had had its fingers in mining at some point, nobody liked the idea of mountain topping. But Remy wouldn't be around to hear how they took the betrayal.

"I'd better go see what else Aunt Vennie wants me to do." He stood, brushing off his knees. "I'll see you later on."

"You know what's good for you, you'll stay out of her way," Don warned him. "Vennie'll have you hauling half of Dwyer down here if you don't watch it."

"That's all right," Remy said. "I don't mind."

"Saint Remy," he heard Frank say as he climbed back up the little hill.

But it wasn't sainthood. It was about not wanting to have a conversation that got so dangerously close to the truth. Not today. And the best way to do that was to follow Aunt Vennie's orders. He loaded up new plastic garbage cans with layers of ice and soda cans. Arranged rows of lawn chairs and hammered iron stakes into horseshoe pits. Hung speakers and lights and fly tape. Hefted coolers and boxes of food and games and prizes.

By the time the family started showing up, Aunt Vennie was running sweat, wiping her face with a fistful of paper napkins, and would collapse sometime after dinner with a big plastic cup of sangria, crying happily over the sad songs played by the country western band she'd hired.

Remy was still following last-minute orders, but he submitted to having his face squeezed by Cousin Amy and his back clapped by various male relatives, hearing his height exclaimed over, his resemblance to his daddy, out-of-stater complaints about "these backcountry roads, six hours from Roanoke. *Six hours!*"

When someone crept up behind him, stretching to put their hands over his eyes but barely reaching with their fingertips, he turned, expecting a younger female relative, and found Dana.

"Surprise!"

Yeah, it was.

"Okay," she said. "I won't ask if it's a good surprise."

"It's just a surprise," he said. Not bad, necessarily, only that it had taken a long time for him to get the picture of her sad face out of his head last night. "Aren't you working?"

"Even a starving artist gets a day off once in a while." She raked her hair behind her ears. "Actually, it's in the terms of my grant. I can only work forty hours a week. Something to do with fair labor or something."

"So you do this often?" Remy glanced around nervously, but

most everyone was still hugging each other. "Crash family reunions?"

"I didn't crash!" Dana protested. "Your cousin Amy practically dragged me along. She met me at the ice machine this morning and got my whole sorry story out of me. She wouldn't hear of leaving me all alone at the Duke of Dee when you were having such a good time here. There's going to be a band and fireworks. I'm actually pretty miffed you didn't invite me yourself."

"Not that many fireworks," Remy said. "And it's a country band."

"What makes you think I don't like country music?" She crossed her arms. "I've got Martina McBride in my car right now."

"Maybe you'd better go crack a window."

"Ha ha. Besides, I'm planning on earning my keep."

She picked up a plastic bag at her feet and held it open so he could see inside. Bottles of colorful paint, brushes, and sponges.

"You planning on painting us a family portrait?" he asked. "Do you have any clue how many Walkers are going to be here today?"

"I'm not painting a portrait," she said. "I'm going to do face painting for the little kids. I drove all the way to Bluefield for the supplies."

"Face painting," he said doubtfully.

"Look." She sighed and closed the bag. "If you want me to leave . . . Uh-oh. Incoming aunt alert."

Remy just had time to glance over his shoulder and say, "Actually, that'd be a second cousin," before he was the victim of another face squeeze.

"That's not Remy! Lordy, you've gotten so tall. Like your daddy!"

Remy tried to break free, but Second Cousin Linda had a grip like a face-sucking alien and moved in for a big, sloppy Passion-scented kill.

"Hi, there!" Dana leaned into the picture, obviously highly amused.

"Linda, this is Dana Shaeffer," Remy said.

"Hello, darling. Is this your girlfriend, Remy?" Linda asked.

"No," Dana and Remy said together, and Dana quickly explained what she was doing there.

"Oh, that's right. We met this morning at the motel," Linda said. "Oh lordy, just listen to Vennie! Someone ought to slip her that sangria now. That woman needs to relax. So then you're still seeing that pretty blonde?" she asked Remy, letting go of his face and wrapping her arms around his middle. "Where is she? Is she here?"

"No, she had to go away for a couple of weeks," Remy said, working his jaw back and forth. "Visiting with a family friend."

"Aw, that's too bad. Oh, there's your daddy. I haven't seen him since the last reunion. I'll talk to you later." She reached and gave Dana's hand a squeeze. "And you enjoy yourself, darling."

"Seriously," Dana said after Linda was gone. "If you want me to leave, I will. I probably shouldn't have come. It sounded like a lot of fun and there hasn't been much of that, lately."

It'd be mean to tell her to go.

"I don't mind," he said. "You ought to stay."

"You're sure?"

"Yeah."

What he wasn't sure about was why he wished she wasn't there, why it worried him to have her around.

She smiled. "I won't follow you," she said. "You go and do . . . whatever it is Walkers do."

He went back to fetching and carrying for Aunt Vennie, but he bumped into Dana often enough to want to take Aunt Vennie's Sharpie and write "Not Remy's girlfriend" on the back of the Walker Family Reunion T-shirt someone had given her. The shirt was three sizes too big, bright green, and clashed with her short pink skirt, but she loudly insisted she loved it and tied it up in a big knot over her stomach.

Remy caught himself watching her, his eye pulled by her slight pink and green body weaving through the crowd of Walkers, laughing with younger cousins, listening intently to great uncles, playing with fat babies, painting unicorns and crowns and light- ning bolts and West Virginia logos on the smooth cheeks of the little kids. She was good with the kids. She was good with every- body.

What was he doing studying Dana anyway? He took himself off down to the horseshoe pits and got into a wild game with some cousins. He was down there when the police cruiser rolled by, but it was only his mom's cousin Terry and his partner, come by for a plate of food. Aunt Vennie piled them up with chicken and potato salad.

"No repeats of the other week?" Terry asked Remy.

"Not in public, anyway," Remy said, then when Terry jingled his handcuffs at him, "Kidding! Kidding!"

He didn't see Dana again until he went back up to the pavilion for dessert. Three picnic tables disappeared under cakes and pies, fruit salad and ambrosia, cookies and fudge. The kids were happy at last, fat little hands stealing hunks of fudge and cookies, grand-mothers feeding babies cake over their mothers' protests. The women who had made the desserts pushed them on anyone nearby.

He was cutting a slice of blueberry pie when Dana sidled up next to him.

"Hey."

"Hey," he said back.

"Did you know your great-aunt Mary was born with three kid-neys?" Dana perched on the end of a table. "No? Well, she was, but now she's down to one. And your cousin Regina thinks we're in End Times because nobody will buy her time share in Boca Raton."

"You have to admit that's a problem."

"And your third—" She considered, a finger on her chin. "I think it was Third Cousin Kyle can recite the preamble to the Con-stitution backwards."

Remy slid his pie on a plate. "I guess everyone in your family is as normal as this pie."

"I'm not making fun of them." She put her hand on his wrist. "I like them. They're sweet. My family wouldn't be as nice to some-one they didn't know and probably would never see again."

She meant it, he could tell. It made her eyes look even bigger and darker.

"There you are, Remy! I was just saying I hadn't seen you all day."

Remy went under to another female embrace.

"Oh my, look at you! So tall and handsome. You favor your mother a good bit."

That was new.

"Dana, this is my second cousin Helen," Remy said.

"Second cousin once removed," she corrected him.

"We've already met." Dana smiled at Cousin Helen.

"Yes, we had a nice long chat," Cousin Helen said. "Have you tried my hummingbird cake yet, dear? You do know why they call it hummingbird cake?"

Dana shook her head.

"Because when you take a bite," Cousin Helen said, "you go 'Mmmmmm-MM!' Here, hand me a plate, Remy." She cut Dana a fat slice. "I use fresh pineapple in mine. That's the secret. Only don't tell Linda. She's always trying to get the recipe out of me." Cousin Helen handed Dana the cake. "Go on, now. Take a bite."

Dana popped a big bite in her mouth. Remy watched her eyes go wide.

"Mmmmmm-MM!" She swallowed hard. "I feel like a hummingbird."

Cousin Helen went away smiling.

"Oh my God, that was like having a five-pound bag of sugar explode in my mouth!" Dana gasped. "Need water!"

Remy dug a bottle of spring water out of one of the drink-filled garbage cans for her.

"No wonder hummingbirds fly so fast," she said. "They're on a massive sugar high."

"It's not a cake for hummingbirds," Remy said. "It's supposed to make you hum. It's a southern thing."

Dana gulped water. "If Cousin Helen makes pit bull burgers or angry mountain lion pie, I don't want to know about it."

"Pit bull burgers?" Remy cocked an eyebrow at her.

"Don't you have relatives to catch up with?"

Remy wandered away, mainly because it felt like there was a limit to how long he could spend with Dana without people wondering. He spotted his dad down at the horseshoe pits. They hadn't talked much since Thursday night, and it hung between them like fog. Remy also wasn't in the mood to find out what his dad thought about Dana being at the reunion, not that there wasn't a perfectly good explanation.

He ended up down by the river, wishing he had a beer. Terry was gone and he was pretty sure no one else would mind. But just as he was about to go get one, Uncle Bernie came and stood next to him. They stared at the river together.

The bank on the other side rose almost vertically to High Street, houses clinging to the edge of the road like they'd just climbed out of the river, everything covered in a thick green blanket of kudzu. The Rope ran below them. Three months ago, it had roared over its banks, tearing up everything in its path. The whole of Bantz Park had been five feet under water. Now it was back to running quiet, clear brown, like pale tea. Hard to believe, when you looked at it, that it could get so furious so fast.

"When I was a boy," Uncle Bernie said to the water, "that river was black as tar. Wasn't no fish or no ducks on it. It was all runoff from the mines. You'd get real sick if you fell in. Now it's pretty again. A success story, the governor calls it."

He turned to Remy.

"So you're leaving."

"Yeah," Remy said before he thought. "How'd you know?"

"Alvin told me. He wanted me to know—about the mountain."

Uncle Bernie was Remy's grandfather's brother, and Remy figured his dad felt Bernie had a right to know what happened to Walker Mountain.

"Funny thing that the river's all cleared up but the people are going," Uncle Bernie said, looking back at the river. "Won't be anyone left to care soon. But if there was something for the people to stay for, the river'd still be black. I guess you trade one kind of success for another."

"I guess."

Remy'd always known a clear brown Rope and a dwindling town. When he looked at the river now, it was only a river. Yeah, it was beautiful, but it was a kind of beauty that didn't even have a price anymore. It was out of reach.

Uncle Bernie's head lifted at the sound of guitars behind them.

"The band's here," he said. "Let's go on and see if they're any good."

"I'll catch up with you," Remy said. "I want to get a drink first."

He walked back to the pavilion and rooted through the garbage can for a drink. Behind him, he heard an out-of-state cousin whose name he couldn't remember arguing with his wife.

"I want to leave now," she said. "The motel is horrible. I'm not going to stay there with my children one more night. We can start now and if we trade off driving, we can go all night and be home by morning."

"We didn't drive the whole way up here just to stay for six hours!" the cousin said. "Momma would have a fit if we left now."

"Momma? *Momma?*" his wife said. "Since when do you call your mother Momma? God, I hate it here. I don't know how anyone can stand living here. It's like being trapped in a bowl."

Remy escaped, trailing down to the stone and cement amphitheater. The sun was sinking behind the mountains, and the lights were on around the stage, throwing the area in front into a little darkness, but Remy could still pick out Dana. She'd shed the green T-shirt and was dancing in front of the stage in her short pink dress. Remy made his way over to her.

"Oh, hey!" she said when she saw him, still dancing. "I've got to tell you"—she pointed at his chest—"the Walkers know how to party."

Her enthusiasm was irresistible. He started matching her steps, and she stood back a little and smiled.

"I thought you were one of those guys who don't dance."

"Not like the guys danced at your party," he said. "This is my kind of dancing."

He took her hands and twirled her so her back was up against him and then spun her around. Her cheeks went as pink as her dress and she laughed.

"I think this could be my kind of dancing, too."

They danced two dances together until the band shifted into a slow song. Remy hesitated, stood on the urge to see what it felt like to hold her close against him. Stood long enough for his cousin Frank to step between them.

"Want to dance?" he asked Dana.

"Sure!" She smiled and slipped away in his arms.

Remy backed away from the wanting to know. It was just curiosity. You didn't have to act on it. He wandered up the hill to the pavilion, looking for something to eat. He felt a tap on his shoulder and turned to see his dad.

"Hey," Remy said. "What's up?"

"Listen, I've had a migraine all day." His dad rubbed a hand up over his face and back and forth across his forehead. "I can't stand it anymore. I need to get home, but I don't want to drive. You mind leaving now and taking me home?"

Remy scanned the dancers, saw Dana was now with a bunch of female cousins who were teaching her some steps.

"Yeah, I don't mind," he said. "Only Aunt Vennie probably wants me to stay and help clean up."

"You done enough for Vennie today," his dad said. "Come on. And let's just leave without saying anything, or it'll take an hour of hugging and kissing to get out of here."

So they slipped behind the pavilions to the truck and climbed in. Remy backed out; his dad sat in the passenger seat, his head on the headrest, his eyes closed.

"Too damned many people asking me about the mountain," he said. "Don't know how that rumor got around so fast."

Only it wasn't a rumor. It was true.

"You sure spent enough time with that Mustang girl today."

"I didn't ask her to come," Remy said. "Amy brought her."

"I know that." His dad opened his eyes a crack, looked at him. "I'm just saying. You spent a lot of time with her."

Remy ground the old truck's gears. "She didn't know anyone else there," he said. "It was just friendly talk." He said it without thinking and it came out so firm, so simple that he felt it must be true. He was almost glad his dad had brought it up. The muscles across his shoulders slackened. He pulled away from the park and drove into town.

"Next reunion," his dad said, his eyes closed again, "you'll be one of them out-of-town Walkers. If you come back."

"Yeah," Remy agreed. He'd be back. But he'd be like an artist who only paints on the weekends.

SIXTEEN

Remy spent Sunday helping clean up from the reunion. When they were done, he didn't much feel like going home. Things were funny still between him and his dad, so he took Aunt Vennie up on an offer of dinner at her house and tried to focus on the fact that Lisa would be back in a week. He felt suspended, caught waiting between her and his dad's visible unhappiness. The thing was done. There was only the waiting to move on. But the waiting burned, like the air was caustic, and it had turned on him, now that he'd decided to leave. He felt his skin being stripped away again and the raw feelings come back.

So it was a relief to go to work on Monday, to have something concrete to think about. An oil change was an oil change, with clear specific steps that yielded predictable results. And that afternoon, Duff declared Cassie road-ready.

"Yeah, you could trick it out a little more and maybe there's some things ought to be replaced," he said. "But for now, you've got a reliable and—I don't mind saying so myself—pretty damned hot engine."

Getting behind Cassie's wheel was the unadulterated best thing that happened in a week. The kind of bursting happiness he'd felt when Jimmy'd first signed her over spread through him, the pressure in his lungs so great he wanted to shout, to laugh out loud. Sitting waiting to pull out on the road, he gunned the engine and this time got a satisfying low roar instead of a coughing death rattle, and he knew he had to give it a real run.

He swung up onto the highway, avoiding town, reveling in the sound of the engine bouncing off the cut rock. When he came up on the water tower and saw Dana putting her paints away, his foot automatically eased off the accelerator and Cassie drifted into the pull-off.

"Hey!" He rolled down the passenger window and shouted.

Dana looked up, annoyed, but the annoyance dissolved when she saw him.

"Hey, back. Sounds great! What did you do to it?"

"We've been working on it, me and Duff." Remy ran his hands possessively over the steering wheel. "I'm taking her out for a real test, see how she does." He looked at Dana, her eyes traveling over the dashboard. "Want to come along?"

Her eyes met his, and for the first time he saw something like uncertainty on her face.

"Really?" she asked.

"Yeah," he said, and then added more surely, "Yeah. It's no fun alone."

"Okay! Let me pack up my stuff."

She locked her things in her car and jumped in next to him.

"Where are we going?" she asked.

"Well, I been thinking," he said, "about you and your water towers. There's a place I think you ought to see. It's a couple of miles down the road, just right for a nice run."

"You're the cruise director." Dana settled back into the seat, and Remy pulled Cassie out.

He drove. In the mountains with roads that curled first one way around half a mountain and then switched back to follow another, it was hard to keep track of what direction you were going, easy to get turned around and feel that you were lost. It was what the tourists and the outsiders complained about, the sense of being trapped and tricked by circular roads and mountain after mountain, some that seemed to float over the roads like heavy green clouds.

But Remy knew McGuire County the way a boy growing up with few restrictions other than his own initiative and energy level can know a place. The roads and where they went and where they came out were mapped in his brain. He knew the roads to avoid, where you could come around a sharp curve and end up run into a gully by a coal truck. Cassie's powerful old engine climbed the steeps better than the whining modern compacts and even the lumbering SUVs they passed.

Dana never squealed or even winced. She sat with her elbow propped on the open window frame, face tipped into the wind. Only when they passed a sign for Greenlea and Remy took the turnoff a little short, Cassie rocking hard to the left, did she grip the seat with her other hand and give him a startled look.

"Sorry." He laughed. "I sort of forgot where I was going."

Greenlea was a settlement on the rail line, not even an eighth the size of Dwyer, hit as hard as every other town by the coal bust, but benefiting by being closer to the Virginia line and a major highway, not quite so lost in the mountains as Dwyer seemed. Greenlea's four intersecting streets and jumble of old company houses had become an artist colony, fueled by a new interest in mountain crafts and partly funded by state agencies. A lot of the small houses were open studios, where you could watch weavers or wood-carvers or potters at their work, with little shops to buy the finished products. Though most of the shops were closed on Mondays.

"Sorry, I forgot about that," Remy said. "They have to stay open on the weekends for the tourists, so a lot of them close up on Mondays for a break."

They walked up the street and peeked through the windows. But at the weaver's, a woman saw them and came to the door.

"You can come on in," she said, pushing back a strand of gray-streaked dark hair. "I've got the big loom set up. I never can seem to take a whole day off."

She stood back to let them pass into her studio, which was most of the front half of the long, narrow house. Three looms of different sizes were parked around the open space, and the woman's work was displayed on tables and racks and hung from the whitewashed walls. Baskets spilled over with big spools of various colored yarns. It was cluttered but clean.

"Saturdays and Sundays are the best times to come," the weaver said. "We do get pretty crowded some summer weekends, but that's when most of us are in the studios working."

"How many artists are there?" Dana asked.

"Right now, there are eight of us. There's a list in here. Tells you the different things we make." The weaver handed her a pamphlet. She moved over to one of the looms and seated herself. "The number changes every now and then."

"Why's that?" Dana followed her. Remy wandered around, looking at things.

"Oh, someone new will come in or someone else will leave," the woman said. "Not everyone can make a go of it. I don't suppose either of you is a glassblower? We could use a glassblower. Everyone wants to make pottery, though."

"I guess you have to sell a lot of stuff to make a living this way," Dana said.

"Well, you never make what some people call a living," the weaver said. "But that's one of the sacrifices you make if this is what you want out of life."

Remy thought he'd heard that before. It's what Lisa had said, making sacrifices to make their plans work. But sacrifices worked the other way. There were sacrifices you could make to stay.

"Have you always lived around here?" Dana asked.

"No! I'm originally from Pittsburgh. But I couldn't take it up there. Too many people getting their elbows in your way. I don't think any of our current residents are actually from around here."

"So how'd you end up down here?" Remy turned his back on a display of place mats.

"Just look around," the weaver said. "If you could pick anywhere to live, anywhere at all, why wouldn't you pick this place? Now come on over and I'll show you how we thread the shuttle."

Remy looked out the side window, opening on a view of Greenlea Mountain, the summer haze softening the familiar shapes of treetops into a great green cloud, rising out of the hollow. And all around them there was the gentle peace of being set apart from the world, the air scrubbed by green leaves and great rocks and quick-flowing streams. Just look around, the weaver had said. But some people forgot to look or never cared for what they saw.

He turned back and watched the weaver work for a few minutes, admiring the swift skill of her hands, almost hypnotized by the rhythm of the shuttle moving through the threads. After Dana bought a handwoven wool scarf and hat, even though the temperature had climbed close to ninety, they left.

"Eventually I'll need them," she said, twisting the scarf around her neck.

They walked along the creek below the town. There was always a creek; they ran through the mountains like capillaries. On the other side, across the railroad tracks, another mountain rose green and unbroken. You could not see from Greenlea—as you could not see from Dwyer or Hager or lots of other mountain towns—that there was anyone else in the world but you. You took it on faith.

Why would you pick anywhere else to live, the weaver had said. Well, there were reasons. Sometimes just loving a place wasn't enough to justify living there.

"The whole time I've been here," Dana said, "I haven't really seen the mountains."

"Um, well, there's a big one right in front of you," Remy said.

"I mean get up in them." She whacked him with her scarf, which had little wooden beads tied on the ends and actually hurt a good bit. "You know, off the road, out of the car and really see the mountains. Except up at Painter Falls, but that probably doesn't count, does it?"

"That's pretty much the Disneyworld version, yeah."

"Then show me the real thing."

"What, you mean take you on a hike?"

"Mm-hm." She nodded.

He squinted at the sky. "It's a little late for a real ramble."

"Just a mini ramble, then."

Why not? It'd delay going back home. Walker Mountain was the mountain he knew best, but he didn't think he could take a pleasure hike over the places he knew like he knew himself. So he drove a couple miles northwest of Dwyer, parked in a roadside pullover, and led her up into the mountains.

At first, he had to admit, he was testing her, setting a pretty stiff pace up the mountain, climbing over rocks, letting her pull herself up, grabbing hold of tree limbs and underbrush. It wasn't easy hiking, but she was athletic and sure-footed and didn't complain. She mostly kept up with him and only laughed at herself when she couldn't. She didn't talk much, either, maybe asking him the names of things, of streams and trees, but no gushing, no faux-nature-girl stuff. Something inside him shifted, pushed aside that feeling of involuntary and not always welcome attraction to her. He found himself liking her. The feeling reinforced what he'd told his dad Saturday night. Friendly talk. He liked her. They were friends.

"You know," she said, punting. "I am putting thorough and complete trust in your knowledge of where the heck we are. You will be able to find the way back, right?"

"No problem." He reached back to help her over some rocks. "We used to come up here a lot when we were kids. There's a great place in the next hollow where Mr. Howard, the owner, would let us dig up wild ginseng. We used to make a lot of money, selling it to this lady in town."

He stopped because stretched across the path were two thin wires, running parallel to each other, as far as he could see in both directions, hung every ten yards or so with yellow signs that read:

Keep Out!
Danger: Blasting Zone
Trespassers Will Be Prosecuted
Mountaineer State Mining Co.

"No!" It came out almost like a cry and without his permission. *Not here,* he thought, staring at the sign.

"What is it?" Dana came up behind him. "Blasting zone?" she read. "What are they blasting?"

He had a bad feeling he knew exactly what they were blasting, but there was only one way to find out. Pushing down on the lower wire with one foot and lifting the other, he slipped between them.

"Um, do you think that's a good idea?" Dana said.

"I just want to see," Remy said, staring up the path into the trees.

"Yeah, but if they're blasting in there, it's probably dangerous." Dana stood on the other side of the wire, dancing anxiously in place. "There could be a reason why it's fenced off, like . . . oh, say . . . to keep you from getting your head blown off or something."

"Wait here," Remy said. "I'll be right back."

"And if you don't come back, what am I supposed to do?" she

shouted after him. "I'll never find my way out of here alone, you know! Do you want that on your conscience?"

"They won't be blasting this late in the day," he called over his shoulder, hoping he was right. It was a stupid thing to do, but he had to find out.

Dana groaned and he turned to see her squeezing through the wires. "Wait for me."

He was too impatient now and headed along the trail. It was a deer path, really: narrow, steep, and rocky, winding through the trees. He heard Dana scrambling behind him, but couldn't slow down to help her. He was driven, pushed and pulled by one frantic thought: what was on the other side of the ridge?

Farther along, he started to notice that the trees and underbrush were covered in a thin layer of fine gray dust, and ahead, the ranks of trees opened up and the green was broken by windows of sky between the tree trunks. And then it ended.

Remy stopped where the forest stopped, standing on what ought to have been the curve of the mountain with the hollow below, and looked down into an alien world.

"It's gone. It's just gone," he said.

He'd seen pictures before. Lots of pictures, but he'd never seen the results of mountaintop removal mining in person. The sea of rippling green clouds that made up the mountains ended abruptly where they stood and before them spread the gray-brown plateaus and gullies of a moonscape. It spread so far that the mountains on the other side were only a misty blue suggestion. The massive dragline—a digging machine the size of a three-story building—was dwarfed by the scale of the altered landscape.

"What happened?" Dana asked, her voice full of horror.

"They mountain-topped it."

How many mountains? Remy wondered. But you couldn't even tell what had been a mountain anymore. The overburden—everything they'd ripped off the tops of the mountains—had filled up the valleys and hollows so you couldn't tell. There was nothing left that he recognized.

"Is this what you were talking about that day?" Dana murmured. "Mountaintop something?"

"Mountaintop removal mining," he said, the words like stones in his throat.

"I can't believe it." She shook her head. "It's horrible."

"It's fast and cheap."

"And they'll just leave it like this?" Dana asked. "Or will they fix it?"

"They can't *fix* it." He couldn't help the bitterness that ate up his voice. "The company will try to restore the land when they've got all the coal, but there's no way they can put it back the way it was."

The Appalachian Mountains were some of the oldest mountains on earth, had once been on the scale of the Rockies, Remy had learned in school. It had taken millions of years to make them into the mountains he knew. And months to blow them apart.

It wouldn't happen to Walker Mountain, he reminded himself. But he felt like something inside him had blown apart, too.

"How can they get away with it?" Dana asked.

Remy snorted, a short, ugly noise.

"Because the mountains don't matter to anyone."

"What do you mean?" Dana asked. "How can they not matter?"

"They just don't. If they did, people would be fussing about this, but they aren't because they don't care." He realized he was shouting and stopped, shook his head. "I'm sorry. It's not like it's your fault."

"It's okay," she said. "I don't know how anybody could look at this and not get mad."

But nobody was looking. And now he couldn't look anymore, couldn't stand there staring down at the total ruin beneath them.

"I have to go," he said, turning his back on the mining site. "I have to go—home."

SEVENTEEN

It was dark when they pulled into the parking lot of the Duke of Dee Motel. Everything was strung with white twinkle lights: the roofline, balconies of the rooms, the fence, the stone wall, the magnolia trees in the garden, even the shed for the ice machine. But nobody was around. It looked a little sad, like a party where no one showed up.

"Arlette's such a kick," Dana said. "All these lights. I really love her. I'm so glad you brought me here and I got to meet her."

Remy didn't say anything, only stared at the light-hung Coke machine.

Dana sighed. "Do you want to come in and talk?"

He shook his head. He just wanted to go home.

"Okay." She sighed again and climbed out of the car. "I'll see you."

He left her standing under the twinkling magnolia trees and headed for home.

The trailer was dark. His dad must already be in bed, he

thought. But no, the pickup was nowhere around. Must have gone out, maybe down to the VFW. Just as well. Remy was glad not to have to talk to him right then. He stumbled into his room and dropped into bed with his clothes on. But he couldn't sleep. He tried thinking about Lisa, counting the days until she'd be back. Tried thinking about their plans. They were good plans. He had to hold on to that. But when he fell asleep, he dreamed about walking through dust. Miles and miles of nothing but fine gray dust.

He woke up around dawn and couldn't stand it anymore, got out of bed quietly so as not to wake his dad, crept out of the trailer by the back door and headed up the mountain. He followed the little unnamed creek up to the foundation of the old Walker homestead. The air was steamy already, draped heavily over everything, like walking through soup.

He sat down on the old foundation and looked out. You couldn't see much in the summer, with the trees all in leaf. In the winter, you could see a couple of the houses on the south end of town. But in summer, you felt like you were alone in a green cocoon, and you had to be okay with that. You had to be okay with a lot of things to settle here. Like working hard all the time, having little, making your own fun. The Walkers brought some of it with them and some of it they learned by living there. Down into the bones and into the way they thought about things, they were shaped so distinctly by this place, like evolution. They were made by the mountains and they'd passed that on to him. That's what he would always have, what he could take with him. It'd have to be enough.

Nearby, where the creek passed the foundation, was a small pool. Remy and his cousin Dylan had dug it out and shored it up themselves, pulling out rocks and arranging them to dam the water. He'd kept it up with some school friends over the years, putting back rocks when floods washed them away and digging the pool deeper and wider. On this suffocating morning, it was too tempting, coolly reflecting back the green around it. Remy pulled off his boots, stripped off his shirt and jeans and slipped into the cold, clear water.

Submerged completely, he felt the sweat and funk and torment from yesterday lifted away. His skin tingled as though something in the water was drawing out all the frustration and confusion. Everything was going to be okay. Don't think. Just feel. He stayed under as long as he could, surfacing with a blustering gasp, shaking water and wet hair out of his face.

"The first time I met you, you were all wet."

He spun around, spraying water, to see Dana sitting on a big rock next to the pool.

"Jesus, you scared me!"

"Sorry." She didn't look sorry.

"What are you doing here?" He stood in water up to his waist, aware that the only thing he had on was a pair of thin boxers. "This early."

"Well, when I got up to go to work this morning," she said, "I realized my car was still at the water tower. I think we sort of forgot that last night, when you dropped me off at the motel."

He hadn't even thought. "I'm sorry. That was my fault. I wasn't thinking."

"It's okay," she said. "The thing is that nobody is around at the motel who could give me a ride, and also, I can't find my keys and I'm hoping they're in your car. So I followed the shortcut over here to find you, but nobody answered the door at your trailer. I saw your car was still there and I saw this path and thought it was worth a shot. And here you are." She took a breath, eyeing him up and down. "Is this some kind of daily ritual thing you do?"

"No."

Now he felt stupid again, like that day they met and she caught him with his head under the spring. It probably wasn't much past six in the morning and here he was, caught frolicking in a mountain pool. How much of a crazy hillbilly did that make him?

"I just needed to cool off," he said. And he was cooling off. Deep under the surface, the water was so cold his toes were going numb. His jeans were on the rock next to where Dana was sitting. "Um, could you maybe turn around so I can get out and put my pants on?"

"You mean these?" Dana looked down at the jeans in mock surprise. She picked them up and grinned wickedly at him. "What a vulnerable situation you've left yourself in, Mr. Walker. I now control your pants."

"Yeah, well. You can either put them down or start walking all the way up to the water tower. It'll only take you about an hour."

"Oh, all right." She wrinkled her nose at him, put the jeans down, and turned her back on him. "This is just like a movie."

"Yeah, Nightmare on Walker Mountain." Remy scrambled out of the pool and snatched up his jeans.

"You really know how to flatter a girl," Dana said over her shoulder.

Remy jerked his jeans over his wet legs and hurriedly snapped them.

"Okay, you can turn around," he said, sitting down on the rock and digging his socks out of his boots. "You see my shirt any-where?"

She found it on the ground behind the rock, picked it up, and handed it to him.

"Are you always this careless about where you leave your clothes?"

"I wasn't expecting company." Remy pulled on his boots.

"Oh, I wasn't complaining!" She perched on the rock again, watching him. "Listen, I wanted to thank you again."

"What for?" He pulled the T-shirt over his head and shook out his wet hair.

"For being so nice to me." The teasing lilt was gone from her voice. "You didn't have to be. I don't mean just getting me the room with Arlette. But taking me to Greenlea yesterday. That was more than helping out someone who was stranded. I don't know if you'll ever know what it meant to me. I could hardly sleep last night."

"I'm glad I could help give you insomnia."

"No, it was good not-sleeping," she said. "I had a lot of things to think about, thanks to you."

"It was no big deal." But he felt his face burn red and crouched down to tie his boots.

"It is to me," Dana said. "I know you think the water tower thing is stupid, but you understood what was important to me. That's why you took me to Greenlea, right? Because you thought it might give me an option."

"I thought you'd like it," he said.

"You thought," she said. "That's what I mean. You took the

time to think and care. That's pretty rare. Do you know what a great guy you are?"

"Wait till you get the bill for my consultation fee," he said, wishing she'd stop being so serious and go back to teasing. Serious was starting to feel dangerous.

"No, I mean it," she said, her eyes wide and warm. "I've known enough jerks that the good ones stand out a mile."

He was just being nice. He was nice to all his friends. He ought to tell her that. But when she sat there looking at him like that, like—like he was everything she thought he was—he knew they were moving onto shaky ground.

"Maybe you're the greatest guy I've ever met."

Remy straightened up.

"We ought to go see if your keys are in my car."

He turned to head down the path, feeling the sudden need to be out of the deep green hollow and into the open air.

"Wait!" Dana stood and grabbed his hand.

He stopped, her touch tingling like the water in the pool.

"God!" The word came from deep in her throat, and she turned her eyes away, not looking at him. "You're going to make me spell it out, aren't you?"

He stood frozen. "What?"

"The real reason I asked you to the cookout, why I went to your stupid reunion. Why Ian kicked me out."

Remy turned around completely.

"I told you," he said. "I don't need to know."

"Ian's not my boyfriend," she said. "He never was. I thought we were friends, but apparently he had different ideas."

"Dana, come on." He tried to gently slide her hand off of his wrist.

"No, listen." Dana grabbed on with both hands. "Ian threw me out because he was jealous, because I was chasing you." Her eyes flicked back and forth over his face. "Don't tell me you didn't know, too. I think I've been pretty obvious."

Looking down at her, a hot jet of blood rose and burned through his brain until he felt like he was swimming in it, reaching frantically for something to hold on to.

"I have a girlfriend," he said. He was going away with Lisa to make a life together. And Dana was offering . . . what?

"But you're the one that picked me up yesterday," she said. "You could have kept driving. You could have told me to go away how many times? Having a girlfriend doesn't stop you from feeling what you feel, does it?"

It was a slap upside the head. Remy pulled his hand away.

"Yeah, I guess," he said, bending down to retie his boot.

"You guess? Whatever you do, don't admit it or anything!" she almost shouted.

"I don't know, okay? I don't know what I think about you."

"That makes us even," Dana said. "Don't you want to find out?"

Remy didn't answer, concentrated on his boots.

"Tell me we're just friends," Dana said. "Tell me you don't think about me any other way."

But he wasn't thinking. That was the problem. He loved Lisa. You didn't cut your heart out for someone unless you loved them, right? And if you loved someone, you didn't stand around arguing about how you felt about someone else. You walked away.

He started down the path, not caring if Dana followed or not. But he heard her footsteps behind him, heard her trip and fall. Remy hesitated a second, then turned around, reaching a hand to help her up. The warmth of her skin melted against his, but her fingers, strong and sure, wrapped around his hand. She was so close he could see the fine sprinkling of brown freckles across her nose and cheeks.

"I don't know what you want." He pushed the words through a throat gone suddenly tight. "You're only going to be here a couple more weeks and then what?"

"I don't know." Her eyes fixed on his like maybe she'd find the answer there.

He realized he was still clutching her hand and let go.

"Because if that's all you want . . ." He was nearly choking on the words now. "Someone to fool around with for a couple of weeks, I can't do that."

She didn't know what was at stake. She was only playing, like she was playing with her life, wanting to make enough money to pay for an apartment because it would be cool. When he was making decisions he could never take back, never change . . .

She reached up and traced the border of his lips with her finger, her touch trembling down his spine. His eyelids flickered, his body wanting to give way, but he grabbed her wrist.

"Dana, stop."

"Why?"

She laid her head on his chest and inhaled deeply. Remy felt her warm breath filtered through cotton, shivered, closed his eyes, but there was no stopping now.

With both hands, he took her head and turned her face to his, bending to her mouth, fingers tangled in her curls. She was warm and soft and her body pressed against his was a thousand times more amazing than he'd imagined—because he had imagined.

Her arms came around him, her hands slowly working their way down his back, following every muscle. Her lips were sweet and her hands were everywhere. His own hands traveled down the curve of her neck and the sides of her body, feeling the way her waist curved out to her hips. He wanted to hold her forever, lay her down by the stream, under the trees, the way he'd done with Lisa—

"Jesus God!" he croaked.

He let her go and stumbled back a step, and a rock inside him split wide open. The rock he'd been building everything on cracked wide like something in the Bible, smote by—what? Knowledge. The knowing poured out of the rock, flooded his mind.

"What's wrong?" Dana reached for him, but he pushed her hands away.

He turned from her, his hands clenched into fists. "I've screwed everything up."

"Screwed what up?"

"Lisa" was all he could say. He couldn't explain the rest.

"*Lisa?*" she said. "If this is about her, then what's the big deal? So you kissed me. Just walk away! Tell me flat out and I'll leave you alone, okay?"

"That isn't it." He wanted to tear something, break something, smash something to bits.

"I don't understand you," Dana said. "You ask me if I'm fooling around, but what about you? What are you doing?"

"I don't know! I don't know! That's the problem." He couldn't make her understand. "I thought I knew what I wanted and that I was doing the right thing . . ." He looked at her and saw her anger-hard face soften. "It was all wrong."

He barely whispered the words, but they felt to him like hard stones flung at glass. Shattered. Everything was shattered. Like the mountains. There was no putting it back together.

"Remy," Dana said. "Give me a clue here. What's wrong? Me? Is it me?"

"No. No, it isn't you."

He wanted to run headlong down the mountain, run until his chest ached from it. But he couldn't leave her hanging. She deserved an explanation, no matter what was crumbling.

"My dad sold Walker Mountain to the mining company."

"What?" she asked, like she hadn't heard right.

"I told him to sell it. He did it so he could give me money to go away." He handed the words to her like broken pieces of rock. "So I could go with Lisa when she goes to college and we could afford an apartment."

"Ohhh . . ." Dana put a hand to her mouth.

"It seemed so right, like it was working out for a reason," Remy said. "When we needed money, there was the offer from the mining company, right when Lisa's parents said they wouldn't pay for an apartment. It was like someone was saying to go ahead."

"You mean they're going to do this mountaintop thing to this mountain?" Dana asked. "Tear it down like what we saw yesterday? And you're okay with that?"

"No, they're not mountain-topping it."

He'd have to go back to the start, explain. So he told her from the beginning, the plans Lisa and he had made, her parents and his dad and the mining company offer, laid everything out for her like she was his judge and jury and could tell him if he was guilty or not.

"I don't know what you want me to say," she said when he was done.

He shouldn't have expected any more from her.

"Nothing," he said. "There's nothing to say. It's all smashed."

"Why? Because of me? Because of what just happened here?"

"No!" Remy took a breath. "It's not your fault. It's my fault. I don't know what I'm doing."

He thought he was in love, the kind that would never change. His stomach twisted with terror, knowing he could be so wrong.

"And yesterday, when we saw that mining site and it was so awful"—he was rambling now—"It was so awful but I thought it would be worth it. It was a trade-off. The mountain for Lisa. Only now everything feels wrong."

"Because of me," she said quietly.

He shook his head, not even sure if he could say what he was thinking, not wanting to hear it out loud.

"I don't know if I love her that much," he almost whispered. "And if I don't, then it's not worth it."

"What I still don't get," Dana said, a tiny edge of disgust to her voice, "is if you pretty much consider yourself married, why did you pick me up yesterday? Why take me places? Don't you think I have a right to read something into that? Like maybe you're more than interested?"

Remy could only look at her helplessly.

"I don't know."

He didn't have an answer for her or himself. The sun was

climbing, lighting up the trees until everything glowed green and he couldn't think.

"Does this really have to change anything?" Dana asked. "Nothing happened. I mean, if you really love her, enough to tear yourself up for her . . ."

In the moving shadows from the leaves, he thought he saw something else cross her face. Something . . . wistful, maybe that was the word.

"Maybe," he said, breathless. "I don't know."

"If you love her, it—" Dana's voice broke, and when she went on, it was flat, defeated. "It won't matter."

But it did. Deep down, under that shattered rock, he knew. It mattered because now he wasn't sure. He needed time to think, but there wasn't time. If everything he felt for Lisa was gone, like it had never even been real, then the mountain was gone for nothing, and there was nothing he could do about it. Was there? He wished he could remember what his dad said.

His dad. He needed to talk to him, find out about the mountain, if he could stop it, at least long enough to figure out what he was doing.

"I have to find my dad," he told Dana.

EIGHTEEN

His dad wasn't home.

"He's probably at work," Dana said. "Can't you call there?"

Remy shook his head. Too much to explain.

"We don't have a phone. And he—he's self-employed."

"Okay," Dana said. "So what does he do and where does he do it?"

"Different stuff. Lately, he's been digging out coal by hand, way back in the mountains."

"Do you know where?"

"I think so."

"Then let's go," she said, her voice full of its usual energy.

"No," Remy said. "I mean, thanks, but I really need to talk to him alone. I'll find him. Let me take you up to the water tower first."

"Are you sure?"

"Yeah."

She had every right to be furious with him, he knew that. But here she was, putting her own feelings aside and trying to help. He could at least get her back to her own work.

She found her keys under the seat of his car, and he drove her up to the water tower, trying to keep down the rising panic of not knowing where his dad was. Maybe he wasn't backcountry. Maybe he'd gone to Bluefield to finalize the sale agreement. Maybe it was absolutely too late.

Dana climbed out of Cassie and stood for a minute with the door open.

"Look, I—" she started to say something then stopped, let out her breath. "Let me know, okay?"

She didn't say what, but Remy nodded.

"I will," he said. He felt terrible, leaving her standing on the side of the road, but he had to find his dad.

He drove back through town, making a huge effort to keep to the speed limit, panic definitely taking over. What had happened? He hadn't pulled away from Dana because he didn't want to betray Lisa. He'd stopped because he'd felt more than just the roaring of his body. He'd felt the possibility of Dana as Dana, as someone who could be important to him, that he wanted to be with and could maybe love. Someone he wanted to find out about.

That feeling had reached inside him and ripped up everything he had built around Lisa. He had thought he was in love, and the cost of believing it was high.

There was no sign of his dad at the mining site. He checked the VFW, his dad's lawyer's office, Loretta's Diner, everywhere he could think of, but his dad was nowhere.

Remy sat slumped at the traffic light at the junction of Route 25 and Route 61. He'd have to go to Bluefield. He couldn't think of anywhere else his dad would be. It was an hour-and-a-half drive to Bluefield, dreading the whole way what he'd find when he got there.

That's when he saw the pickup come down the long drive from the Duke of Dee and turn on 61 toward Walker Hollow. When the light turned green, Remy gunned Cassie's engine and raced through the intersection, following the truck back home.

"Thought I heard someone right behind me," his dad said as he climbed out of the pickup.

"I've been looking everywhere for you!" Remy slammed Cassie's door and stalked over to his dad. "Where *were* you?"

His dad drew his brows together. "What do you mean, where was I? I was at Arlette's. We went out last night and I had a couple of beers and she didn't want me to drive home, so I stayed at the motel. Since when do I have to tell you my every move?"

"Since I couldn't find you when I had something important to tell you!" Remy couldn't even begin to think about the news that his dad had spent the night at Arlette's. He'd have to set that aside for later. "You could have let me know. I was all over town. I went the whole way back to your mining pit. I've been going crazy."

"Well, you weren't here when I left," his dad shouted back. "And I didn't know where you were, either. So I guess we're even."

They stood for a second, glaring at each other and breathing hard, then his dad said, "What was so all-fired important you had to hunt for me all over town?"

Remy suddenly felt paralyzed, couldn't ask because he was afraid of the answer. Don't let it be too late. So he stood there and watched his dad dig a cigarette out of his pocket and light it, guarding the flame with his hand.

"Well?" his dad mumbled around the cigarette.

"I don't want to sell the mountain," Remy said, the words rushing out.

His dad's eyes opened wide, and he sucked in his breath, choking on smoke. Coughing a little, he stood there, looking at the ground, his shoulders shaking. For an awful moment, Remy thought his dad was crying, but when his dad looked up, he was laughing, shaking his head and laughing, though he didn't look particularly happy.

"I wish I knew what was going on in your head."

"That makes two of us," Remy said.

"Look, Remy," his dad said and sighed. "I got nothing for you. If I don't sell this mountain, what are you going to live on? You're gonna go to Pennsylvania and get some dead-end job that'll kill you inside. This way, you'll have a chance to do the things you want to do."

"It isn't worth it," Remy said and told his dad what he and Dana had stumbled on the day before, only he left out mentioning Dana being with him.

"I know you saw something pretty terrible at the mining site yesterday, but what can we do? If coal is what keeps this state going, what can we do about it?"

"We can hang on to what we have."

"Nah." His dad shook his head. "This is the one thing I can do for you, and I'm going to do it."

He took a drag on his cigarette, blowing the smoke up toward the sky. "Come on in and I'll make us some breakfast." He started toward the trailer, but Remy didn't follow him.

"I'm not going to Pennsylvania," he called after his dad's back.

His dad stopped, turned, not laughing this time.

"Okay, you want to let me in on what's going on?"

"I'm not leaving," Remy said. "I'm not going with Lisa. I changed my mind."

His dad came back, pointing a finger at Remy.

"This have anything to do with that Mustang girl?" his dad asked.

"No, it doesn't have anything to do with Dana."

Remy realized as he said it that it was true, as stupid as it seemed. He hadn't shifted his feelings to Dana. Dana had been like a glass that showed you things in a different way when you looked through it. And even though his mind was full of grand, new, important ideas and dread of things that must be done, just saying her name was something grand and new all on its own.

But his dad wasn't buying it.

"It ain't your mind that got changed," he said. "It was some other body part."

"I know it looks that way," Remy said. "And yeah, I like Dana and I'm interested in her, but it isn't about her. She won't be around much longer, then she'll be going back to school. I'm not planning on following her."

He paused, surprised by his own thoughts.

"I'm not following anyone anymore."

It felt like a declaration.

His dad stared hard at him. Remy felt his eyes trying to bore him down, but he kept his head up, his own eyes steady.

"It's not what I want," he said, measuring each word. "I want to stay here. I belong here."

"So how can you be sure you're thinking right this time?"

"I don't know."

Remy looked down, caught sight of the black coal tattoo above his hand, the letters R.A.W.

"It doesn't make me feel raw inside," he said.

"Lots of people would say that ain't a good enough reason," his dad said. "Lots of people would say maybe you're afraid of leaving what you know for what you don't. I know because they said it about me, too."

"Were you scared?" Remy looked up, looked at his dad's lean, lined face, the graying beard making him look older than he really was.

"Never thought I was," his dad said. "Some people feel different things. Like most of my cousins felt the pull to go and see other things, but I felt the pull to stay. I don't know why. Maybe I was never as curious as they were. Or never dissatisfied. But I never felt scared."

Remy watched his eyes travel around their home: the trailer, the barren garden, the mountains.

"Hell, boy. I never shielded you from the way I lived. You think a scared man would willingly take on a life like mine?"

"It's been my life, too," Remy said. "And it never scared me."

"Lots of people leave, Remy," his dad said. "It ain't wrong if you ain't happy here. Like your mom. She wanted more than she could find here, and that's okay."

Remy already knew that he didn't want the things his mom wanted.

"I'm not Mom," he said.

"And I don't want you to worry about me." His dad's voice hardened. "I don't want you to feel like you're tied to this place for any reason. Don't pick the wrong reason to leave, but don't pick the wrong reason to stay, either. You gotta find what's going to make you happy."

"I'm not leaving," Remy said again, firmly, surely.

They were quiet, both of them looking at the mountain that had its imprint in everything that had made them. His dad threw his cigarette in the dirt and ground it out with his heel.

"Is it too late?" Remy asked.

"I don't know," his dad said. "The papers I signed were just to agree not to accept any other offers. They weren't a final signing over of rights. I'll have to see. Have Johnston look at them tomorrow." Johnston Davis was his lawyer. "Come on." He jerked his head toward the trailer. "Let's go have some breakfast first, then we'll work this out, somehow. Between the two of us hardheads, we ought to be able to figure it out."

They walked side by side to the trailer, and his dad dropped an arm across Remy's shoulders.

"Listen," Remy said, "don't keep saying you don't have anything to give me. What do you think you've been doing for the last seventeen years?"

A slow smile spread across his dad's face.

"Going steadily gray," he said.

"You know what I mean." Remy smiled back. "We've got more to hang on to than this old mountain."

NINETEEN

Lisa came home the next Monday. He waited for her after work on the steps in front of her house, his insides churning, wishing for some other way to do this. He had loved her, even if that love had changed. Even if what he'd felt hadn't been undying love, it had been strong, and it made him want to treat her fair.

Seeing her coming across the steep lawn from Mrs. Hambro's house, he waited to see what would rise. Used to be that just watching her made his heart crash against his ribs, amazed that she was his. Now it only made her seem unreal, like she was already part of another world.

Dread prickled down his spine, even as she threw her arms around him and pressed her cheek against his, making him shiver in the heat.

"It's so good to hold you!" she whispered in his ear. "I missed you so much!"

He had put his arms around her because he felt like he had to, but it seemed like such a lie. Still, he couldn't just break away from her. Instead, he put his hands on her shoulders and held her away from him.

"I have to talk to you," he said, the words dry in his mouth.

"I know!" She was practically dancing. "I have so much to tell you, too. Let's go somewhere."

She took hold of his hand and tried to pull him off the steps, but he stayed where he was, dragging against her pull.

"Come on!" she urged.

"No, wait a minute."

"What's the matter?" Lisa stood in front of him, her eyebrows knit together in concern.

He had to tell her, here and now, or he wouldn't be able to do it. He'd lose his nerve, give in and go ahead with their plans.

"I'm not going," he said. "I can't go with you."

"What?" Her smile was uncertain. "Quit fooling around."

"I'm staying here. I'm not leaving."

"What are you talking about? Everything's fixed now. As soon as we get the money we can go, like we planned."

"I'm saying I don't *want* to go. I—I changed my mind."

"Are you serious?" she whispered.

He nodded.

"What happened?" she asked. "Is it your dad? Did he change his mind about the money?"

"No," Remy said. "It was me. I'm sorry. I can't let him sell Walker Mountain. I just can't. So I told him not to sell it."

She was quiet for a minute, working it out.

"Well, okay," she said. "That doesn't matter. So your dad

doesn't sell the mountain. That doesn't mean you have to stay here. We can make it work somehow. We'll figure it out."

"No, listen." Because she didn't seem to be hearing him right. "This doesn't have anything to do with my dad. I *want* to stay." He realized he was still holding her hand and let it go. "I'm sorry."

She cradled the hand he'd let go like it was broken.

"Why?" she asked, tears gathering in her eyes.

"I belong here." And when he said it, he knew it was the simple truth. "Everything that's important to me is a part of this place. I can't lose that."

"What about me?" Her voice cracked with pain. "I thought you wanted to be with me."

He couldn't look at her anymore, so he stared at his boots. It was worse than when he'd told his dad he was leaving. Worse almost than anything except that moment when he thought he'd lost Walker Mountain.

"Remy?" Lisa prodded him with her voice. "Don't you want to be with me?"

She was almost pleading, making him look at her, see the tears sliding down her face, see how bad he was hurting her.

"No," he said quietly. "I'm sorry."

She recoiled like he'd hit her.

"What happened? I don't understand. What did I do? You weren't like this when I left! What happened?"

"I don't know. It wasn't anything you did. I just—" How could he explain it to her? "Some things happened that made me think, and I knew I was making a mistake."

"Is this about Dana?"

"What?" Remy was so startled he couldn't think. "No! She doesn't have anything to do with it."

"She does!" Lisa was almost shouting. "Don't lie! Bree told me she saw you and Dana in your car, but I didn't think it meant anything. Did it?"

Remy screwed his eyes shut. He didn't want to have to talk about Dana, didn't want Lisa to think Dana was the clear and simple reason for everything when it was one big tangle and he didn't know where Dana fit in.

"It doesn't have anything to do with her," he said.

"You're *lying*!" She punctuated the word by shoving him hard in the chest. "It's all a lie! All this crap about 'I belong here' and blah blah blah, when you've been cheating on me!"

She came at him again, and he tried to grab her hands but she beat him away.

"What do you think is going to happen now? If you think she's going to stay here, you're crazy!" She stood on the sidewalk and took a couple of hysterical breaths. "I can't believe this! I can't believe my parents were right about you!"

She put her hands over her face and sobbed, shoulders bent and shaking. Remy felt like he was on fire, burning up right there on the steps in front of her house.

"I'm sorry," he said, stupidly. Helplessly.

"Stop saying that!" she wailed. "Get out of here! Leave me alone!"

She ran past him, up the steps and into the house, slamming the stained-glass door so hard that Remy waited to hear it shatter.

He slumped against the stone wall, his back to the house, stunned. It felt like he'd had a hole ripped through his insides. A hole where something warm and comforting had been curled up for a long, long time, and now it was gone. He'd ripped it out himself.

He'd loved Lisa. Maybe he still did—a part of him, anyway. Enough that he hated himself for what he'd done to her. *Do you know what a great guy you are?* He heard Dana's voice in his head. Great guys didn't hurt nice girls the way he'd hurt Lisa. But he didn't know what else he could have done.

He went slowly down the sidewalk to Cassie and climbed in. Sitting in the stuffy heat, he closed his eyes, wondering what he should do now. Finally, he couldn't take the heat anymore, started Cassie and pulled away.

Remy kept his head down for the rest of the week, working and going home, avoiding places he might run into Lisa, but mostly waiting on edge to see if his dad could get out of the sale contract for the mountain.

He hadn't seen Dana since the morning they'd kissed almost two weeks ago. She hadn't come by the garage, and every time he passed the water tower, it seemed like there was someone else there talking to her. She had gotten pretty well-known around town and had attracted a group of admirers. They had things to say to each other, but Remy didn't want to say them in front of a crowd. Problem was, he didn't know how much time he had before she finished up with the water tower and moved on. It didn't seem fair that she'd have to go before they even had a chance to figure things out.

But finally, on his way home from work that following Monday afternoon, there was only the red Mustang parked at the water tower. He pulled in behind it and got out. Up on the ridge, the heat bounced off the highway and the rock wall behind it, hotter than that day five weeks ago when he'd stopped to put his head under the outfall of water and Dana had called to him. But if his palms were sweaty, it wasn't from the heat.

"Hey!" Dana sidled around her scaffolding and waved at him. "I thought I heard a well-endowed car coming this way."

"I knew I picked the right name for her," he called back.

He crossed over to stand below the scaffolding. She sat on the rough plank, leaning on the rail, her paint-spattered boots swinging in his face. Remy squinted up at her, his hand shielding his eyes.

"Haven't seen you for a while."

Dana shrugged. "I've been working hard. I need to get this thing done."

"What are you painting up there?" he asked. "The Last Supper?"

"I had a couple of changes to make," she said. "But it's pretty much done."

She folded her arms on the scaffolding and rested her head on them, her face more uncertain than he'd ever seen it.

"Why?" she asked. "Are you wishing I'd go?"

She could be direct when she wanted. Remy knew that. He shook his head.

"No."

"Good." She smiled. "Because I wasn't sure, after the other week. I figured I'd better back off a little."

"I guess I freaked you out pretty bad?" he asked.

"No!" She sat up. "I mean, I was worried about you, yeah, but mostly I was ashamed of myself. It wasn't exactly my finest moment. I don't normally chase guys up mountains."

"That's good," he said. "Because not everyone finds that a turn-on."

She swung her foot at his head, and he dodged it.

They were quiet for a minute. Remy shifted his feet on the gravel.

"So you've got your own fan club now," he said. "Always someone hanging around here, talking to you."

Dana perked up. "I know! People have been super nice to me," she said. "Look what someone brought me today." She held up a half-empty container of iced tea. "I don't have to worry about going into town for a drink anymore. People bring me things. It's amazing. I could get used to this."

"Too bad we don't have any more water towers for you to paint," Remy said. "I guess you'll have to move along soon?" He already knew the answer.

"Yeah." She nodded. "I have *got* to get my rear in gear. I have two more of these things to do before school starts."

"Oh, right." She had to go back to school. There wasn't really any hope for them. It was over before it ever really had a chance to get started.

"You'll be leaving soon, too," she said, and for a minute he couldn't figure out what she meant until he remembered that she didn't know.

"Nah," he said. "I'm not going anywhere."

She frowned down at him, her chin on the scaffolding. "I thought you were going with Lisa? The mountain was sold and everything."

"My dad's working on breaking the deal with the mining company," he said. "I changed my mind about leaving. I'm going to stay here."

"I'm glad." Her hands clasped the railing. "About everything, but I'm really glad you're not going to let the mining company tear up your mountain. I'll never get that image out of my head, what we saw that day."

"Yeah," Remy said. "It won't stop them, but—you know—at least I'm not making it easy for them."

"What happens now?" she asked. "You get to keep your mountain and then what?"

"Duff says there's a continuing education program that would pay for me to get my mechanic's certification over in Felter," Remy said. "It's too late to apply for the fall semester, but maybe I can get approved by January."

"That sounds great. I hope it works out." Feet swinging gently, she stared down at him. "Hey, come on up here a second. I want to show you something."

"Show me what?" He felt safer talking to her from the ground.

"Just something." She pulled herself to her feet. "Come on. I won't bite you."

"I'm not afraid of being bit," he said.

"I won't push you off the mountain, either," she said. "Come on up."

Remy climbed the scaffolding and heaved himself up on the rough boards next to Dana. The water tower wasn't especially big, but the view from the ridge was downright dizzying.

Seen from the tower, Dwyer looked as if it had tumbled down the mountainside, into the valley. So surrounded by green, it wouldn't take much for the trees to reclaim it, cover up the houses and buildings like some lost jungle temple.

Remy turned to Dana's mural. It was different now from the sketch she'd shown him. The once-anonymous mountains now matched the horizon that surrounded Dwyer. She'd kept Rosella Banks, but Senator McGonaugle had been replaced by a fiddle player who looked kind of like a member of the band from the reunion.

"Well? What do you think?"

He looked at Dana and back at the mural, trying to fit the two together. He didn't know why he was so surprised. From seeing her sketches, he knew she was good. But this—this was something else entirely.

"It's good," he said. "Really good. You're really good."

Dana smiled. "Do you think it looks like you?" she asked, a little anxious.

At first, Remy couldn't understand what she was saying. He stared hard at the mural until he saw it, saw his own face staring back from the face of the coal miner. The rest of the miner—the lantern helmet, the broad shoulders that definitely weren't his, down to hands holding a lunch pail and a pick—didn't look familiar. But the face was his. He thought of the sketch—still in the shoe box under his bed—but that was only a suggestion of his face compared to this. Not just that it looked like him, like a photograph. It bared him, almost like she'd put his whole summer's struggle up there for everyone to see.

The first unconsidered thought was a hot dart of anger at her, like she'd taken something from him, and he felt a sudden sympathy with Stone Age tribes who didn't want missionaries taking their pictures and ran them through with spears. Only he couldn't run Dana through with a spear.

He turned to her and was going to say something smart about the size of his hands, but she was looking at him funny.

"Yeah, it really looks like me," he said. "Except I never thought I'd get to be a coal miner. But you never know, do you?"

"So you like it?" She sounded relieved.

Now he could get smart with her.

"I like the proportions. You know what they say about the size of a man's hands."

"Oh, you're a pig!" She smacked him on the shoulder, but she was smiling.

Remy stared at the miner with his face, still with a strange sense of having been lessened. He wanted to ask her to take it off, to change it, but it would sound crazy. Or just plain mean.

"I wish it was enough," she said. "I wish my dad was wrong, but I don't know. It scares me to think I might not be able to do the thing I want to do the most."

Remy tore his eyes off his painted face and looked at Dana, feeling a hundred years older than her.

"Maybe it depends on what your idea of enough is."

"Maybe it does," she said. "Maybe I don't have to want what my dad wants."

"Maybe."

"We don't all have to live the same way." Her eyes were still locked on his. "Until this whole country turns into one big suburb and strip mall and everyone's exactly alike. How boring would that be?"

"I don't even want to imagine." He grinned.

"Me either." Dana appraised her own work, tilting her head. "I keep thinking about that weaver at Greenlea. She seemed pretty happy about the choice she'd made."

"Yeah, but I bet it wasn't easy," Remy said. "It's probably not for everybody. They always have a couple of empty studios because people give up and go back."

"At least they tried," Dana said.

He took a breath, tried to make what he was going to say sound casual, a suggestion.

"You could try."

"I've thought about it," she said, crossing her arms. "It's a huge leap, though. I really want to finish school, first."

"No, I mean just try," Remy said. "Like a trial. Like next summer, maybe they'd give you a summer lease on one of the studios so you could see if you like it, see if people like your stuff."

She turned to look at him again, and this time her eyes were lit up.

"That's an amazing idea," she said. "I would love that! To be able to do what I want to do all day would be fantastic. Do you think they'd let me do that?"

Remy shrugged. "I have off tomorrow. If you want, I could take you over there, talk to some people."

"I do want. Thanks."

She gave him a knockout smile and he was thrown back to that very first day, down on the road and the sudden urge to grab her and kiss her.

"And you know," he said casually. "If you come back next summer, I'll be here. We might even run into each other every once in a while."

"We might," she said. "I'm getting pretty good at climbing mountains."

If he stood there much longer, looking at her, he was going to have to do something about it, and the water tower wasn't exactly the right place for that.

"I gotta get going," he said, climbing down off the scaffolding. He needed to find out if his dad had heard anything yet. "I'll stop by the motel around nine, okay?"

"I'll be ready. Where are you off to now?"

He smiled at her.

"I'm going home."

ACKNOWLEDGMENTS

As corny as it sounds, writing Remy's story was a journey and anyone who knows me will believe it when I tell you that I would have given up long ago and sat down by the side of the road and cried if not for the help of so many along the way. And so I owe a great deal of thanks to the generous fellow writers who offered invaluable critiques, suggestions, and support; you ladies know who you are. Thank you to the Wyatts of Welch for making me feel like family. To my editor, Janine O'Malley, and the many wonderful people at FSG. And most especially to Paul Rodeen for never losing faith in this story and Andy Wyatt for never losing faith in me and for patiently answering every stupid question about cars that I shouted down the hallway. And to Tom Petty for providing the soundtrack.